T0129209

Someone's Mad
at the Hatter

Books by Sandra Bretting

MURDER AT MORNINGSIDE

SOMETHING FOUL AT SWEETWATER

SOMEONE'S MAD AT THE HATTER

Published by Kensington Publishing Corporation

Someone's Mad at the Hatter

Sandra Bretting

LYRICAL UNDERGROUND
Kensington Publishing Corp.
www.kensingtonbooks.com

LYRICAL UNDERGROUND BOOKS are published by

Kensington Publishing Corp.
119 West 40th Street
New York, NY 10018

All Kensington titles, imprints, and distributed lines are available at special quantity discounts for bulk purchases for sales promotion, premiums, fund-raising, educational, or institutional use.

Special book excerpts or customized printings can also be created to fit specific needs. For details, write or phone the office of the Kensington Sales Manager: Kensington Publishing Corp., 119 West 40th Street, New York, NY 10018. Attn. Sales Department. Phone: 1-800-221-2647.

Lyrical Underground and Lyrical Underground logo Reg. US Pat. & TM Off.

First Electronic Edition: October 2017
eISBN-13: 978-1-60183-717-2
eISBN-10: 1-60183-717-8

First Print Edition: October 2017
ISBN-13: 978-1-60183-718-9
ISBN-10: 1-60183-718-6

Printed in the United States of America

Chapter 1

Maybe it was the sight of so many eyes swimming around the stockpot that bothered me. I couldn't exactly scoop up the black-eyed peas when they squinted like that. Not to mention the sauce was full of garlic, jalapeños, and onions, which made my nose itch. Whatever the reason, I walked past the pot of good-luck peas on the mansion's buffet table and headed for a stack of sweet milk biscuits instead.

"Missy! Over here." Ambrose waved to me from the other side of the dining room.

I grabbed a biscuit and crossed the room, which was easy, since Mr. Dupre's New Year's Day breakfast had thinned and only a few folks remained.

"Where've you been?" he asked. "And aren't you gonna try the peas?"

"Not this early in the morning." Unlike me, my best-friend-turned-beau had a cast-iron stomach. "I've been here awhile, but I ran across Beatrice and we wanted to catch up."

My assistant, Beatrice, and I had been invited, along with half of Bleu Bayou, to usher in another January at the old Sweetwater mansion, Southern-style. Along with black-eyed peas, the buffet held breakfast tacos laced with collard greens, which folks swore would fatten your wallet, and omelets filled with roast pork, which was another tradition Southerners held near and dear. Not sure how that one started, since it involved pigs and the way they rooted forward in the mud, but, as my granddaddy used to say, "Traditions are what put the sugar in sweet tea."

So, come January first, everyone loaded a Chinet plate with

cooked greens, fried pork and swimming peas, and hoped for the best.

Ambrose shook his head. "You're missing out."

"It's early. I want to give my stomach a chance to wake up first."

He flashed me a crooked smile, which made my heart flip-flop. We'd only recently begun to date, after wasting a perfectly good year and a half as friends and housemates, but my heart couldn't help the palpitations.

His lopsided grin quickly faded, though. "Say, something happened a little while ago. I took a phone call from one of my clients, and she's panicked. Gained fifteen pounds over the holidays and now she's afraid her wedding gown won't fit. I promised I'd meet her at the studio for another fitting."

"Today? But it's New Year's Day!" I popped a biscuit in my mouth. After spending so much time designing wedding gowns for persnickety brides, Ambrose deserved a holiday. Not to mention, I'd created enough hats, veils, and fancy headbands to crown every bride from here to the Louisiana border. I quickly chewed and swallowed. "Can't it wait? We never take time off. I was hoping we'd spend the day together."

"Sorry, but it can't. She's paying me fifteen thousand for the gown."

He pecked me on the cheek, and the palpitations began again. *That man always does know how to shut me up.* "Okay. Do what you gotta do."

"I'll be home soon." He held up his hand. "Promise. I'll give her one quick fitting and then I'll head back to our rent house."

Ambrose and I shared what the locals called a "rent house." Although we each had our own bedroom, I hoped one day we might share a *whole* lot more.

"Sounds like you've already made up your mind," I said. "Please come home at some point, though. I know how you get when you're with a client."

"I will." He held up his hand again. "I swear. It'll be a couple hours, max. And I've got a great idea. Why don't you go to your hat studio in the meantime? You can pick up your mail and maybe double-check the locks."

Well, that doesn't sound so bad. I'd been meaning to stop by Crowning Glory over the holidays, anyway. But, somehow, I never made it out of fuzzy socks, tattered Vanderbilt T-shirts, and faded yoga pants, which wouldn't be the best advertisement for my business.

Today was different, though. Today I wore a Brooks Brothers blazer, wool pencil skirt, and brand-new boots, so maybe I should make the most of it. "Okay, okay. You're probably right."

He passed me his plate. "I know I am. And here. Eat some peas while I'm gone. I want you to have good luck too."

I accepted the leftovers halfheartedly as he walked away. The fact we stood in this beautiful dining room struck me as lucky enough. Only a few months ago, a greedy property developer tried to snatch the mansion from its heirs and convert it to high-end condos until a local realtor rode to the rescue. If not for him, we might've been standing in a sales office instead of a formal dining room built in the 1800s.

Speaking of which . . . where was he? Usually there was no mistaking Mr. Dupre, what with his colorful dress shirts in their crazy colors.

I quickly scanned the room. Someone in a riot of purple and gold stood across the way, near the kitchen, with his back to me.

I padded over to him. "Good morning, Mr. Dupre." The colors swirled as he whipped around.

"Hello there! And please call me Hank. Mr. Dupre's my dad. Happy New Year!" Instead of shaking the hand I offered, he grabbed me in a big bear hug.

"You too," my voice squeaked.

When I recovered, I noticed someone else was standing nearby. The old woman wore a flour thumbprint in the cleft of her chin.

"Did you cook for us today, Miss Ruby?"

"*Oui*. Da cornbread and collard greens." She spied the nearly full plate in my hand before I could do anything about it. "And ya barely touched yers. Gah-lee. Ya be gettin' so skinny, betcha don' even throw da shadow." She leaned in close. "I gotta magick potion put soma dat weight back on ya."

"I'm sure you do." Everyone in Bleu Bayou knew about Ruby Oubre and her magick potions. She cooked them up in a singlewide she kept on the banks of the Atchafalaya River. Her specialties included love potions, court-case spells, and gris-gris, which was a traditional voodoo charm.

"Ma oil will put da fat back on ya." She clucked her tongue. "Make yer shadow come 'round."

"I'm sure it would. But something came up and I should get going." I turned slightly. "Thanks again for inviting me...uh, Hank."

"You're very welcome." He nodded at the window. "And be careful out there. Last night's rainstorm left the roads real slick. Don't drive too fast."

"I won't. See you both soon."

As I ducked into the kitchen, I spied a silver garbage bin by the back wall. Good luck was one thing, but eating stone-cold peas was quite another, so I carefully tipped Ambrose's plate into the trash before dashing out the back door.

A cool wind feathered my face the minute I stepped outside. Once I drew the flaps of my blazer closed, I joined a gravel path that led from the back of the mansion to its front, pebbles crunching beneath my feet. Normally, a majestic pin oak blocked the property from the street, but the cold had stripped the tree bare and exposed a line of cars parked grille to fender on the road's shoulder.

Most of them I recognized. One, a battered pickup surprisingly painted pink, was pushed into the gleaming bumper of a Rolls-Royce Silver Shadow parked in front of it. Since the pickup belonged to Beatrice, my assistant, I should've been mortified, but the cold urged me to forget about anything but finding my car.

I'd parked my VW all the way on the end, so I rushed to it and fumbled with the door handle until it swung open. Thankfully, the engine started right away and I drove from the mansion under a blanket of wet, gray sky.

Soon a blurry stretch of sugarcane fields materialized in the windshield, the ground littered with leftover stalks from the fall harvest. Most folks picture antebellum mansions when they hear about the Great River Road, but they forget it's mostly fields and petroleum plants that dot this part of the Mississippi River. It's understandable, since the farmland and factories can't possibly compete with the beautifully restored wedding-cake mansions sandwiched in between them.

A few minutes later, I passed the kitschy neon sign for Dippin' Donuts, where a lighted arrow shot from the roof and pierced the sky.

As I passed, I began to mentally compose a to-do list of all the things I wanted to accomplish once I reached my hat studio.

First, I'd scoop up the mail that puddled behind the front door. Next, I'd answer a river of e-mails that no doubt flowed into my computer. Not to mention, I owed several people phone calls, including my accountant, my largest supplier, and the building's landlord. Since that last person had promised to fix a water stain on my studio's ceiling, I mentally moved him to the top of the list.

And while I didn't have any appointments booked for today, I could always leave a few reminder calls for brides coming later in the week.

As soon as I arrived at work, I swerved my VW convertible, which I'd nicknamed Ringo—since it *was* a Beetle, after all—into the main parking lot. The landlord provided a separate lot for us employees behind the shops, but the blacktop on that one spit dirt and tar everywhere, which wouldn't be good for Ringo's undercarriage.

I'd discovered this building by accident. Two stories tall and made of thick, weathered bricks on the outside, the original hardwood plank floors still covered the inside. Everyone called it the Factory because the building once housed a hot-sauce plant. That was before the Tabasco companies all hightailed it out of here, except for the most famous one, which still operated out on Avery Island.

Somewhere along the line, an architect added a soaring glass pyramid between my studio's wing and the one across from it to give the building a modern twist. Sort of like that glass prism at the Louvre, which rose smack-dab from the middle of buildings made centuries before it.

I pulled onto the parking lot, which was mostly empty, and parked next to Ambrose's Audi. Once outside the car, I began to make my way to the studio. Normally, it was a straight shot, but today I hopscotched over puddles slick with leftover motor oil. Apparently, the storm had even ripped a downspout from the wall, and it blocked my path like something tossed there by the Tin Man.

Curious now, I paused. If last night's storm could pull a metal downspout clear off a brick wall, imagine how much damage it could cause my roof. The watermark had appeared overnight on a stand-alone section of ceiling that jutted out from the building. The stain seemed to grow and grow, until it reached the size of a Thanksgiving turkey platter.

A call to my landlord definitely was in order. Although . . . he might be more willing to fix it if I could report the actual amount of rainfall. Maybe I'd even embellish the total a bit, although that didn't seem like a very Christian thing to do. Either way, I had a perfect tool for helping me build my case.

A few months back, I'd stumbled across a page on Pinterest, the mother lode for do-it-yourself projects, which explained how to make a homemade rain gauge from a wood base, an ordinary dowel, and a glass vial from the hardware store. Since "I cain't-never-could," as we say here in the South, resist the urge to fluff things up a bit, I faux-painted an old hat stand for the base and substituted a ribbon curler's handle for a plain dowel. Then I painted fat raindrops on a clear tube from Homestyle Hardware and voilà—I'd made a custom rain gauge with an artful twist.

I'd set the creation on a curb in the employee parking lot, right behind my studio. Just in case, I'd also rescued an old whiskey barrel from the trash heap and rolled it nearby for a second opinion. One look at those two, and I'd know how much rainwater to report.

So I rounded the building and came across the empty parking lot, which wasn't surprising, since everyone else had probably stayed home with their good-luck peas and cornbread. I hugged the back wall and sidestepped more puddles until I reached the curb behind my studio.

Something was wrong, though. My beautiful rain gauge was gone, and the barrel that normally sat next to it lay on its side. Who'd steal a rain gauge? And, more importantly, how could a few inches of water upend a heavy whiskey barrel like that? I stopped in front of the barrel, where I bent to take a glimpse inside.

A lock of hair flowed from the cask onto the asphalt, like a trail of salt poured over pepper. Not only that, but blood matted the strands.

The scream I let loose no doubt sounded four states away.

Chapter 2

Once I finished hollering for all I was worth, I rose. While I wanted to scream again, odds were good no one would hear me, so what was the point? Even Ambrose wouldn't notice the noise, although his studio sat right next to mine.

Unfortunately, Ambrose became as deaf as one of his mannequins whenever he began to work. I'd once seen Bo ignore a shrieking fire alarm, for heaven's sake, because he couldn't figure out how to pleat something correctly. The culprit in that case turned out to be a faulty battery, but *he* didn't know it at the time.

No . . . as much as I loved him, Ambrose couldn't help me now.

I shakily rose, and then I stumbled away from the barrel and settled onto a different curb. Maybe if I closed my eyes and ignored the cask, it'd go away. *One Mississippi, two Mississippi . . . three . . .* My eyes popped open as I turned. *No such luck.* There lay the cask, tipped over like a giant's bath toy, flush against the curb with nowhere left to roll.

Only one thing would make it go away.

I reached into the pocket of my blazer and pulled out my cell. About a year-and-a-half ago, I met up with an old childhood friend when someone murdered one of my clients at a nearby plantation. Lance LaPorte was a detective on the Louisiana State Police force, and together we figured out who killed Trinity Solomon the night before her wedding.

Amazingly, only a year after that, I landed smack-dab in the middle of a different crime scene. That one involved a former sorority sister who'd met an untimely end in a musty garden shed. My fingers stalled over the keypad now. *How can I call Lance again?* He was either going to think I had the worst luck in the world or that crime followed me around like an angry rain cloud. Either way, he'd be dumb-struck when he found out why I was calling.

I steeled myself for his questions and tapped the screen to reach his cell phone. After it rang once, though, I lost my nerve again. What if he wasn't even home? He could be anywhere, what with the holidays and all. Maybe he'd left town or forgot to charge the battery on his cell phone or tucked it somewhere hard to reach. The odds were stacked against me, but I managed to let the call go through without any interference and silently prayed he'd answer the call.

The good Lord answered my prayer on the third ring.

"Missy DuBois! Happy New Year!" He sounded overjoyed, as if he'd been waiting for my call all morning.

"Hey, Lance, I'm *sooo* glad you're there."

"How was your Christmas? Did Santa Claus—"

"Uh, Lance? I hate to interrupt you, but this is *not* a social call."

"No? Then what's up?" His voice dropped, as if I'd sucked the joy right out of him.

I glanced at my rain-soaked barrel. "First, you have to promise me something."

"Now you're freaking me out. Are you in trouble?"

"Not exactly." I took a deep breath and then slowly exhaled. "Okay, here goes. No lectures, please. And promise you won't think I'm cursed. But I may have found another body."

After an hour or two of complete silence, he finally spoke. "What do you mean, you *may* have found a body?"

"That's what it looks like to me."

Another round of silence.

"Well . . . aren't you gonna say something?"

"Hmmm. I didn't see that one coming. No, siree. I mean, what are the odds, right?"

"Agreed. Just my luck I'd find another corpse."

Amazingly, he chuckled. "Wait a minute . . . you're not pulling my leg, are you? Kind of like a New Year's Day joke? You'd better not be—"

"Of course not!" This time I didn't mind interrupting him, since he was talking crazy. "Who in their right mind would pull a stunt like that? Honestly, Lance. You know me better than that."

"Guess you're right. Okay, then." Now his voice turned serious, as if he'd flipped a switch to turn from friend to policeman. "Start at the beginning and tell me everything. Where are you and when did it happen?"

I didn't take offense at his clipped tone, since he was only doing his job. "I'm at work. Got here a little after ten."

"Did you go there alone?"

"Yes. Ambrose is here, but he came a few minutes before me." Hearing Lance take charge made me feel about a hundred times better, so I rose from the curb. "I came here to do paperwork, but I wanted to check on last night's storm first. When I went to the employee parking lot . . . there she was. She'd been stuffed into an old whiskey barrel."

"How'd you know it was a girl?"

"I saw the hair. Long and blond."

Lance gave a low whistle. "Interesting. Did you see anyone else come or go? Or hear anything unusual?"

"No, nothing." I shook my head, although he couldn't see me. "There's no one else here. It must've happened right before I got to the building. I only wanted to check my rain gauge—"

"Uh, Missy? Save it 'til I get there. Right now I need to call a unit to your building. Don't move, okay?"

"Where am I gonna go?" The thought of leaving never even occurred to me. How could I abandon the person I'd found, whoever she was?

Suddenly, my eyes widened. "Oh, shine!"

"What now?"

"What if it's someone I know? It could be anyone. Maybe someone from the building." I clutched my waist. "Or a friend. I didn't see the hair that closely. My gosh, Lance. What if I knew her?"

"Okay, calm down." He'd definitely switched into cop mode. "Get ahold of yourself. There's nothing you can do right now. Stay away from the victim and we'll be there in a few minutes."

I pressed the phone to my ear, since his voice calmed my nerves. "Do you have to hang up?"

"'Fraid so. But I'm calling for the unit now. Just hold on 'til we get there."

"Please be quick."

He hung up and I stumbled toward the next curb in the lineup. It was all I could do to keep myself from throwing up.

What I needed was a hand to hold, a friend to calm me down.

Even though Ambrose might be with a client, he'd come to my aid if I called. I fumbled for the cell and clumsily hit the button for Ambrose's Allure Couture. Like Lance, Bo answered on the third ring.

"Hey, there." His voice was ebullient too, since he had no idea what I'd been through.

"Ambrose?"

"What's wrong?" he quickly asked. "Where are you?" One word from me changed everything.

"I'm in the employee parking lot at our building."

"Say no more. I'll be right there. And don't move."

Why do people keep telling me that? I couldn't move any more than the body in the barrel could up and walk away. "Okay."

The phone tumbled into my lap. An eternity later, something sounded behind me and I turned to see Ambrose, who raced around the building as if his feet were on fire.

He ran even faster when he spied me. He plowed forward and then dropped next to me on the curb, his face wild with worry. "Missy." He wrapped his arms around me before I could even speak.

We stayed like that for a minute or two, until he gently pulled away.

"Okay. What happened?" he asked. "You look like you've seen a ghost."

I silently pointed at the rain barrel.

"What's that?" He eyed the cask. "And how'd it get there?"

"It's a rain barrel. And it's mine."

His eyes slanted, as if I'd answered in Swahili. "I don't get it. Why's it turned over like that?"

"There's a body inside. I found her this morning."

He didn't respond, which only amplified the sound of dry leaves rustling in a nearby chinaberry tree.

"Well, aren't you going to say something?" I asked.

Finally, he found his voice. "No wonder you're so pale. You poor thing. But you know what we have to do, right? We have to call your friend. The one who works with the police department. Here . . . give me your cell. Is he in your contacts?"

I shook my head instead of offering up the phone. "No, we don't have to do that. I already called him and he's on his way. He told me to wait here."

Right about then, a siren overrode our voices and the dry sound of leaves rustling. Ambrose rose from the curb first, and then he helped me up.

It was Lance's dirty Oldsmobile, which zoomed toward us with a strobe light flashing on its roof. The lights turned off when the car skidded to a stop and Lance jumped out.

"Are you okay?" Today he wore a baggy green sweater and wrinkled khakis instead of his usual police uniform. A handsome African-American, a shadow of stubble dappled his cheeks.

I nodded weakly. "I'm okay now. Ambrose kept me company. She's over there." I jerked my thumb at the barrel, which probably wasn't necessary, since it was the only whiskey barrel in the parking lot.

"Okay. You might want to stay put." He pulled a pair of latex gloves from a back pocket and walked around his car's bug-splattered grille. When he reached the cask, he crouched in front of it and instantly stuck his hand into the opening. No doubt he wanted to check for a pulse.

We watched him work for a minute or two, until something else pierced the air. It was another siren, and it grew louder as a Louisiana State Police car screeched into the parking lot.

Instead of making a beeline for us, though, the cruiser first careened over to a dumpster, where a uniformed officer jumped from the passenger side. Once he cleared the car, the officer behind the wheel continued, until the unit pulled up alongside Lance's car.

"C'mon. Let's step over here." Ambrose gently led me to a spot near the wall, but I couldn't resist peering over my shoulder as we walked.

The officer behind the wheel looked oddly familiar. Black crew cut, freshly shaven, with caramel skin. Of course . . . it was Officer Hernandez. The same policeman who responded to my 911 call when I discovered the body of an old sorority sister at Sweetwater.

He hopped from the squad car and strode over to Lance, his gaze glued to the rain barrel. As he crouched beside him, he began to speak in low, urgent tones.

I tried to read his lips, but my attention waned when someone else shouted. The other officer, the one who'd jumped from the cruiser by the trash bin, came running through the parking lot with something in his hands. Whatever it was, he held it at arm's length, as if it might detonate, and he didn't stop running until he reached his coworkers. Then he held up his treasure for everyone to see.

"Here you go," he hollered. "Buried under some newspapers."

I gasped. The officer held a chunk of wood painted the same French blue as my rain gauge.

Everyone turned to stare at me, but Lance spoke first.

"Could you come here, Missy?"

It wasn't a question, so I reluctantly ambled over to where they stood. I didn't dare glance at the hat stand, which was splattered with blood.

"Officer Paschal found the murder weapon in the trash," he said. "Do you know anything about it?"

"Yes. It's mine. I made it."

"Do you want to tell us about it?" His voice was curt, as if we were strangers, for goodness sakes. He didn't sound like someone I'd grown up with and he sure didn't sound like a friend.

"I don't know how it got there; I swear. I placed it on that curb—" I frantically pointed "—about a month ago. I only checked it once or twice."

"So you have no idea how it got in the trash?"

"No, none." I reluctantly glanced at the hat stand. Splashes of crimson streaked its base. "Wait a minute." My mind raced as I struggled to make sense of it all. "That's fresh blood. I just got here. I was at a party at Hank Dupre's this morning. Call him . . . he'll vouch for me."

Lance and Officer Hernandez exchanged quick looks, and then the younger policeman turned away.

"We'll do that." Now Lance's tone was soft. "I need you to come with me to the station, though, to give your statement. I'll drive. Ambrose, you're free to go."

Ambrose and I locked gazes, neither of us willing to leave each other. He looked numb, which was understandable, since I felt exactly the same way.

Chapter 3

After an hour or so in the interview room at the police station, I finally sagged back into the regulation armchair. I tried not to think about how many criminals had slumped against the very same cushion, or whether they'd stared at the same blank walls.

Obviously, the good folks at the Louisiana State Police Department didn't believe in adding color to a room. The walls were beige and the furniture included a putty-colored desk, a white clock with skinny hands, and an unframed two-way mirror. A video camera perched in the far corner.

Since there was nothing else to look at, I closed my eyes and gave my statement to Lance and the blinking video recorder. I included everything: the flour thumbprint on Ruby's chin, the pea gravel that bit into the soles of my brand-new boots, the way the barrel lolled on its side in the employee parking lot. By the time I finished and re-opened my eyes, it was noon, according to the bald-faced clock. *That can't be right.* It felt like days had passed since I'd found an upended rain barrel that dripped blond, bloodied hair.

After a moment, Lance clicked off the video camera. "We're all done. Since you have an alibi, you're free to go. Want me to drive you back to your studio?"

Numbly, I shook my head. *That's the last place I want to be.* "I'll go home. My assistant will come and get me."

"You sure?" Lance looked confused. He probably wondered why I didn't phone Ambrose first.

"I'm positive. And Ambrose deserves a break after everything that happened this morning. I'll let him be for a while."

"Suit yourself." Lance waited for me to rise and then he followed behind as I left the interview room.

We passed putty-colored file cabinets and a few more regulation armchairs on our way through the station. When we reached the front counter, Lance popped open a swinging gate with a hidden button, while I whisked out my cell. Thankfully, Beatrice, my assistant, answered on the second ring once I tapped the number for my hat studio. She'd mentioned wanting to get some work done once she left the New Year's Day breakfast.

"Crowning Glory. May I help you?"

"Hey, Beatrice. It's me."

"Missy? Where'd you go this morning? I looked for your car after the party, but you'd already gone."

I took a deep breath. "It's a long story. The bottom line is I'm here at the police station, and I need a ride home. Can you come get me, please?"

"Of course." She didn't hesitate and she didn't ask a million questions, which made me so grateful that I decided to add a fat bonus to her next paycheck.

"Thanks, Bea. I'll wait for you in the parking lot." I clicked off the line and returned the phone to my pocket.

"Are you sure you want to do that?" Apparently, Lance had been eavesdropping on my conversation.

"Do what?"

"You might be more comfortable if you wait here in the lobby." He threw me a hopeful smile. "I'll keep you company. It's not like you've done anything wrong, you know."

"No?" My tone was icy. "You acted like I was guilty before. Like you didn't believe me when I said I didn't know how the body got there. It's me, Lance. Missy DuBois. We've known each other forever." I didn't mean to bark at him, but he'd worn out my patience with all the police rigamarole.

"Whoa. Hold on." He raised his hands in protest. "You know I can't play favorites. We needed an official statement, since it was your rain gauge we found at the scene."

"I know that, Lance. You don't have to state the obvious." A little voice in my head told me to shut up now, before I said something we'd both regret, so I swallowed my words and turned away.

"I'll call you later." He spoke to my retreating back.

"Yeah, right." Once I reached the exit, I threw open the plate-glass door and barreled outside. My heart pounded against my chest, but, little by little, the thumping subsided and I approached a stone bench near the curb.

I plopped onto the seat and laid my hands in my lap. *Might as well get comfortable, since there is no telling when Beatrice will arrive.* I rested my weary head on the makeshift pillow and closed my eyes.

"You-hoo! Missy!"

Lorda mercy. Please don't let it be who I think it is. I cocked open one eye. Sure enough, Prudence Fortenberry came sailing through the parking lot, as if it was a concert stage. Tall and thin, the reedy pianist wore a boxy faux-fur coat and matching hat.

As soon as she reached me, she tottered to a stop, as if she might fall into the orchestra pit otherwise. "Whatever are you doing here?" she asked.

"Hi, Pru. I'm just resting. Love the hat." I threw her a sweet smile, since it was best to stay on Prudence Fortenberry's good side. I learned the hard way what could happen if you didn't.

It happened a few months ago, when I suggested to a client that "Jesu, Joy of Man's Desiring" was a bit overplayed. Little did I know it was also Prudence Fortenberry's favorite song. She came unglued when the bride struck it from her playlist, and she snubbed me for weeks afterward, referring all her contacts to another hat-maker way up in Baton Rouge.

I quickly found out she had more contacts in this town than a stray cat had fleas. Now I treated Prudence with kid gloves and bit my tongue whenever she said anything ridiculous.

"Is that real fox?" My only hope was to distract her so she wouldn't ask why I was at the police station.

"No, it's not. Why'd you say you're here again?" Apparently, she couldn't be swayed so easily.

"I didn't say. But if you must know, I met up with an old friend this morning. He works as a detective."

"How nice for you."

"And why are *you* here?" I asked. My guess was to complain about something or other to the chief of police, but I could have been wrong.

"I got popped for parking in a handicapped spot." She rolled her eyes. "You wouldn't believe how picky they are about that. As if I didn't have a million other things to worry about."

"You don't say. Guess you should hop to it, then, and go inside to pay your bill."

"It's a horrible way to start the morning, if you ask me. You'd think they'd give me a break, since I'm an artist and all." She clutched at the coat's collar with her long, thin fingers. Although Prudence was as phony as the faux-fur coat, she had the most elegant hands I'd ever seen.

Hallelujah—someone new drove into the parking lot at that moment. It was Beatrice in her pink pickup, which rolled through the entrance like a giant slug.

I quickly rose. "Gotta go, Prudence. Good luck with the parking ticket." I waited for Beatrice to pull over, and then I hiked up my skirt and jumped into the cab. "Thanks, Bea. You're a real lifesaver."

"No problem." She waited for me to close the door before pulling away from the curb. "What did Prudence Fortenberry want?"

"To irritate me, but that's nothing new." I glanced at the rearview mirror and saw Prudence and her ridiculous coat sashay into the station.

"Okay, next question," Beatrice said. "Why are you at the police station?"

"You wouldn't believe me if I told you." Since word, no doubt, would spread through town like wildfire, I might as well confess to my part in the fracas. "I found a dead body behind our studio today. She was stuffed in that whiskey barrel I use to catch the rainwater."

"Lorda mercy!" Beatrice jerked sideways. Thank goodness we hadn't pulled onto the road yet and there was nothing for her to hit but a few curbs.

"There's more." I glanced into the passenger-side mirror again—just in case—but Prudence was long gone. "Do you remember the rain gauge I made from an old hat stand?"

"Of course. You were so proud of that thing. Why?"

"Someone used it as the murder weapon, and then they tossed it in the trash."

She whipped her head around again. "You're kidding!"

"Stop doing that, Beatrice! At this rate we'll never make it to my house in one piece. And why would I kid about something like that?"

"Sorry. That's not what I meant to say. But you caught me by surprise."

"Think about how I felt." I sighed and leaned against the seat. "Can we just drive now?"

"Whatever you say, boss."

We pulled out of the parking lot and, after a mile or so, Highway 18 appeared. Neither of us spoke, but, every once in a while, I caught Beatrice sneaking a peek at me.

After a few more miles, she couldn't take it anymore. "They seriously can't think you had anything to do with the murder. Can they?"

"I don't know. That's what I want to believe." But that was before I saw a shadow of doubt cross Lance's face back there in the interview room. It flickered from one of his ears to the next, and that small moment cut me to the core. Probably because he and I spent every summer of our childhoods side by side, playing marathon rounds of Chinese checkers, slapjack, and crazy eights. How could he doubt me now?

"I don't know what to think anymore," I said.

Once we'd driven another mile or so, we reached Grady's doughnut shop, with its familiar neon arrow on the roof. About a half-dozen cars sat in the parking lot, including Grady's, as the arrow blinked away.

"Are you hungry?" Beatrice glanced at me again. Since her pickup couldn't do more than forty miles an hour, we practically crawled past the shop.

"I don't think so. To be honest, I just want to go home."

"No problem. Course, I haven't asked you the most obvious question."

"I know what you're going to say." No need for her to voice it. "But they wouldn't tell me the victim's name. I only know the girl had long, blond hair."

"That could be anyone. I hope we didn't know her."

"Me too. Look, do you mind if we stop talking about it? It makes me picture the blood in her hair when we do."

"No, of course not." Her chandelier earrings jostled when Beatrice ran her finger across her lips. "I'll keep my lips zipped."

"Thanks."

We fell silent again as we passed the doughnut shop and arrived at the sloping lawn of the Sweetwater mansion. The curb was empty now, the cars long gone, but tire treads marked the watery pea gravel.

Which reminded me of something else. "Say, did Mr. Solomon give you a hard time about parking so close to his Rolls-Royce this morning?"

"You saw that?"

"Well, it was hard to miss. I can't believe you were brave enough to mess with him like that."

She shrugged. "I didn't have anywhere else to park. You know, he's still mad at my uncle for buying the Sweetwater place. The only reason he went to brunch this morning was to spy on him."

"Hmmm. Can't imagine what those two talk about. But I'd love to be a fly on the wall when they do."

She chuckled as we finally drove up to my rent house. "You and me both. Say . . . do you want some company? I don't see Ambrose's car."

I shook my head as she parked, and then I swung open the cab's door. "No, that's okay. He'll be home sometime this afternoon. Right now, all I want is some peace and quiet and maybe a hot bath."

"Okay. But I'd take tomorrow off if I were you. Unless you want people to come around to the store and pester you with questions."

I paused. Maybe she was right. By now, half of Bleu Bayou would know about the murder, and they'd tell the other half by dinnertime. That was the curious thing about living in a small town: There were so few people, but so many opinions.

I couldn't help but bristle at the thought, though. "I don't want to lock myself up in the house. I'll go stir-crazy. Besides, I have a big meeting tomorrow. It's the wedding planners' association, and I haven't seen those folks since before the holidays. At some point, they're going to forget about Crowning Glory if I don't go to their meetings."

The Southern Association of Wedding Planners met only once a month, and it just so happened the January meeting was right down the road at Morningside Plantation. At least a hundred people would be there, including some I'd never met. How could I pass up a chance like that?

"Suit yourself." The earrings jostled again as Beatrice tilted her head. "But I think you're making a big mistake."

"Maybe they won't even know about the murder. Not everyone is from Bleu Bayou, you know." A girl could hope, anyway.

"Sure," she said. "And this old pickup will win at Daytona next year."

"Aren't you supposed to make me feel better? FYI: You're not. And you never know, maybe Lance will find a suspect by then. That way people won't have to make one up."

"Whatever you say, boss."

I wearily hopped out of her truck. "See you tomorrow."

"By the way . . ." She leaned over the seat and peered through the passenger window. "Did you ever eat any of those black-eyed peas at the party this morning?"

"Nope. I never did."

"Maybe you should do us all a favor, then, and have some for dinner."

Chapter 4

The next morning dawned cold and clear. Once I'd retrieved my car from the Factory, I spent the night before talking to Ambrose, purposefully dancing around the subject of the dead girl in the parking lot. After a glass—or was it three?—of wine, I finally slumped off to bed around midnight.

Maybe that was why the earthy smell of Community coffee, which wafted from a travel mug I placed in Ringo's center console for the drive to work, smelled especially good this morning.

I gathered my hair into a high ponytail, lowered Ringo's soft top—since it was the first rain-free morning we'd had in a while—and purposefully took side streets and back alleys to reach the Factory. I even popped a Harry Connick, Jr. disc into the CD player and let the opening notes of "One Fine Thing" wash over me.

My somewhat-good mood immediately soured, though, as soon as I arrived at the Factory. Parked smack-dab in front of the building was a white news van for KATZ, the local ABC affiliate. The van's windows were down and its passengers gone.

My heart raced. As much as I needed to get back to my shop and a normal routine, I couldn't handle a reporter so soon after yesterday. I glanced at the rearview mirror and then threw the convertible into reverse, the sound of Harry's crooning fading beneath my growing panic.

Why didn't Beatrice call to warn me? Obviously, KATZ knew about the murder. The reporter was probably camped out in the employee parking lot at that very moment, or—worse yet—by my studio's front door.

I shoved my hand into the center console and yanked out my cell, which was wedged next to the travel mug. The screen showed I'd missed three calls. *Ouch.* Two of the calls were from Beatrice and one from Ambrose. No doubt I couldn't hear the ringtone over the music.

My mind swirled as I drove back onto the street. Along with missed calls, I'd noticed the time on the phone's screen. It was only nine, which was an hour too early for the wedding planners' meeting at Morningside. But, since I couldn't go to work, maybe I should head over to the plantation anyway. I seemed to recall the hotel kept an ewer of sweet tea on a sideboard in the registration cottage, not to mention a workstation where people like me could plug in a laptop or cell phone while they waited.

Even though I wasn't staying at the plantation overnight, maybe I could crash there until the meeting began. I pulled onto Highway 18 and then waited for the wind to die down a bit before I reached for my cell again.

Thankfully, once I punched in the number for Crowning Glory, Beatrice answered right away.

"Where are you?" she hissed.

"I'm on Highway 18, headed for Morningside."

"That's good. You *don't* want to come here."

Her tone sent shivers pinballing down my spine.

"I know . . . I saw the news van in the parking lot. What in the Sam Hill is going on over there?"

"You're not gonna believe this, but the station sent out Stormie Lanai." A whoosh of air sounded over the receiver as Beatrice shifted the phone from one hand to the other. "She's even worse in person. I swear she's wearing three layers of makeup."

Oh, shine. Stormie Lanai was the investigative reporter for channel 11, not to mention its weather girl, traffic reporter, and all-around gaffer. Her signature sign-off included a cheesy wink that always set my teeth on edge.

"Did she come into the studio?"

"Of course. But she only stayed for a minute or two when she found out you weren't here. Said something about coming back at noon. You might want to disappear for a while."

"Will do. I've got nothing to say to her, anyway. Why doesn't she talk to the police?"

"She did, but my guess is she wants to film her news report here. She kept saying the studio had such 'wonderful color' . . . whatever that means."

"Great. That's just great." No doubt Stormie had grabbed a hat stand when she got there and practiced a few swings for her news report. Why didn't she just audition for a soap opera instead of the five o'clock newscast? "Okay, if the reporter tries to come in again, meet her at the front door. Don't let her get inside. Maybe she'll get bored and go back to the station."

"I don't know, Missy. She almost drooled on me when she saw all the hat stands around here. But, I'll try."

"I know you will. And I'll pick up your call next time too."

I clicked off the line and tapped the screen for Ambrose's studio. After filling him in on my comings and goings, I said good-bye and slid the cell into my pocket.

Soon, the entrance for Morningside Plantation appeared on the road ahead. *Hallelujah.* My mood couldn't help but lighten again at the sight of the gorgeous mansion and its rolling emerald lawn. Two stories high, with frosted white paint and a creamy marble staircase, it practically floated above the grassy knolls. If not for a black iron handrail that tethered the staircase down, it might have blown away with the first good headwind.

It'd been more than a year since I last visited Morningside. That was when I created a one-of-a-kind veil for a society wedding with the rich Solomon clan out of Baton Rouge. The night before the big event, though, a maid discovered Trinity Solomon's body in a downstairs bathroom. She'd been poisoned and left to die on the cold marble tile.

Hopefully, people's memories from that horrible time had dimmed, which seemed to be the case, since cars now filled the hotel's parking lot. I cruised past car after car until I found a spot in the next-to-the-last row, where I parked and hopped out of Ringo.

Once again, my feet landed on rough pea gravel as I joined a path that wended to the registration cottage. Today, though, I wore sensible black flats, which I'd paired with a wraparound dress and an orange cashmere sweater. Although people insist redheads like me should shy away from the color, I like to think orange complements my green eyes and light skin.

The door to the registration cottage swept open easily, and I stepped inside. Everything looked exactly the same. The same desk held a giant Dell computer, catercorner to a sideboard stocked with an ewer of sweet tea. Even the stack of brochures next to the ewer hadn't changed. The only difference was the person standing behind the registration desk. Since Herbert Solomon had bought the place and fired its entire staff, a new general manager now stood watch over the front office.

"Hello, Missy!" A huge grin split Vernice Ficklin's face. Her tanned skin was the color of wheat berries, even in the middle of winter, and her teeth shone like the fluted columns outside.

"Shut my mouth and call me Shirley!" I ran to the desk to give her a quick hug. "Don't tell me: Mr. Solomon gave you the general manager's job!"

She happily hugged me back. "I only applied for it because you said I should."

Which might've been true, but it was neither here nor there at this point. "You deserve this job. Anyone who could turn a profit at the Sleepy Bye Inn will go over like gangbusters here."

She finally released me. "Ain't that the truth. But I'm only the assistant general manager. For now."

"Nothing says you won't be promoted."

She grinned. "You know, the Sleepy Bye Inn is still open. Don't know how they stay in business, what with that dime-store furniture. So, what brings you to Riversbend?"

I scooted over to the sideboard and the ewer of sweet tea. "I'm here for the wedding planners' meeting." I spoke over my shoulder as I plucked a Styrofoam cup from a stack. Then I turned to place it under the spigot and watched brown liquid fill the cup. "They invite vendors like me to their meetings."

"I've seen your work in the newspaper." She tsked a few times. "They always mention Crowning Glory whenever there's a big to-do around here. You must be working overtime."

"Most days. And I hope it stays that way." I rapped my knuckles on the wood sideboard after turning off the spigot. "Say, do you mind if I plug in my phone and answer some e-mails while I'm here?"

"Not at all. We keep two or three different cords by the outlet, so find one that fits. You know where it is."

I edged closer to the wall, trying to balance a full cup in one hand and my phone in the other. Somehow, I managed to plug the phone into the right cord without spilling a drop. But the minute I rose, someone barreled through the front door and made a beeline for the registration desk.

Lorda mercy. I gasped as a girl rushed past me and tea sloshed everywhere. The fireball didn't even pause to look back at the commotion she'd caused.

"Whoa, nelly," Vernice said. "You almost ran down Miss DuBois."

Finally, the stranger stopped and shot me a look. She wore sky-high Manalo Blahniks and a back-combed ponytail every inch as tall as her heels. "Sorry about that. But this is an official emergency."

Vernice cocked her head. "May I help you?"

"We need a projector screen brought to the Magnolia Room. Stat."

Stat? I grabbed a cocktail napkin from the sideboard to wipe the cup clean. "What happened? Does a doctors' convention need an emergency PowerPoint presentation?"

Vernice chuckled. "I think we have a screen somewhere. How long do you need it for, honey?"

"Long enough to show some pictures of one of our members," the girl said. "She was a wedding planner, but someone killed her yesterday." Her eyes opened wide, as if she couldn't believe it.

"Excuse me?"

She glanced over at me. "It's true. And you'd think they'd give the first vice president for conferences and committees—that's *moi*— more time to plan a tribute after something like that."

Can it be? The trickle of blond hair that flowed from the cask? "Are you talking about the body they found yesterday?" My voice was soft. "At a place called the Factory?"

"Yes."

"Who was it?" I asked.

"Charlotte. Charlotte Devereaux. We're all devastated, of course."

I swayed, even though no one had brushed past me this time.

"Are you okay, Missy?" Vernice shot out from behind the counter and clasped her arm around my waist.

"No. No, I'm not."

The stranger squinted. "Did you know Charlotte?"

"Yeah, I did. We worked together."

While we weren't best friends or anything, I got to know her pretty well over the past year and a half. Charlotte also rented a studio at the Factory, and she sent plenty of clients my way. I tried to reciprocate and even recently recommended her to one of my contacts. Willowy and stylish, Charlotte was a product of Riversbend and its Catholic schools here. *Who would do such a thing?*

"I'm afraid it's going to be a terrible shock to our members," the stranger continued. "Not to mention we'll have to fill her committee spot, which isn't going to be easy."

Vernice gave a tight smile. "Let me see about getting you that projector screen."

Thank goodness Vernice spoke first so I wouldn't have to. Imagine worrying about such a trivial detail like a volunteer committee at a time like this! The girl had no sense, not to mention any shame.

"Thank you," the girl said. "Oh, and we might need some more sweet tea. You wouldn't believe how people guzzle that stuff. Just charge it to our account." With that, she tottered away on her designer heels.

I wiggled away from Vernice. "Can you believe that girl? Of all the things to worry about at a time like this! She didn't even mention Charlie's poor family or friends."

"Some people have no horse sense." Vernice shook her head as she returned to the registration desk. "Try not to let her get to you. I'm sure your friend was a wonderful person."

"She *was* wonderful. She and her cousin had this business called Happily Ever After Events. She did all the wedding planning and he handled the accounting." I racked my brain for her cousin's name but came up empty. "He must be devastated. Anyway, I'm sure going to miss Charlotte."

Vernice tentatively pointed to the phone on her desk. "I'm sorry, Missy, but I have to get that screen delivered to the Magnolia Room. With my luck, that girl will throw a hissy fit if I don't move fast enough."

"You're probably right. Speaking of which . . . is it okay if I still hang out here until the meeting starts? I know you've got work to do, so I won't distract you."

"No problem. Really . . . I don't mind. But you might be more comfortable over at the mansion. They delivered some new couches for the lobby, and they look really comfortable."

"Okay. Maybe I'll do that. But I'll stop by here afterward. I want to find out all about your new job."

She chuckled. "There's not a whole lot to tell yet. But I'll be here this afternoon."

Once Vernice fell silent, I backed out of the office and stepped onto the walkway. The morning air immediately cooled my cheeks, which had warmed during the conversation with the callous stranger.

Little did I know when I first arrived at Morningside that someone would confirm my worst fear. Not only did I know the person who'd been stuffed into my rain barrel, but I *liked* her. I liked her a lot.

Which meant Lance had to hurry up his investigation. Anyone who could murder a sweet woman like Charlotte Devereaux didn't deserve a single day of freedom.

Since we hadn't spoken since yesterday, I decided to place a call to the police station. I pulled the cell from the pocket of my sweater, tapped the screen, and waited for him to answer.

"Uh, good morning."

He sounded hesitant, no doubt because of our little spat yesterday.

"Hey, there." I grimaced, thankful he couldn't see me. "Sorry about what happened yesterday. Guess I got a little mad at you."

"That's okay. I should be the one to apologize."

I started my trek toward the mansion, sidestepping puddles along the way. "No, it was my fault. You were just doing your job."

"But I never doubted you for a minute. You have to believe me, Missy. It bothered me all night long I didn't tell you that."

"Yeah, our conversation bothered me too. Why don't we call a truce?"

"Deal. How're you doin' this morning?"

I continued to amble down the path, the mansion in my sights. "I could be better. I found out the victim's name."

"I figured you would. I was gonna call you later. Did you know her?"

"Umm, hmm. We worked together sometimes. Everyone around here loved her. Everyone."

The silence that followed was thick with meaning. If so many people loved Charlotte, our unspoken words implied, then why would someone kill her?

"I mean, she had a spotless reputation," I rushed to explain, even though Lance hadn't asked. "This is gonna hit people really hard around here. Charlotte was one of them."

"So I've heard. Say . . . the coroner will start on his autopsy today.

Might get a preliminary report tonight, if we're lucky. It all depends on his caseload."

"Do you have any leads?"

"A couple. But nothing I can talk about just yet. I'll let you know if one pans out."

"Thanks." Although he hadn't really promised me anything, it was a start. Last summer, when I found out about my client's murder, Lance barely gave me any information. That all changed, though, when I solved the crime and helped out the victim's family, who I happened to know. Even six months ago, when Ambrose and I found Mellette Babineaux lying face down on a dirty concrete floor, I had to move heaven and earth before he'd give me a tidbit of information. But, once again, my sixth sense kicked in and I figured out the person responsible for that crime too. Maybe Lance realized he could trust me now. I sure hoped so, for Charlotte's sake.

"Have you gone back to your studio?" he asked. "I heard that reporter from channel 11 was out there this morning. What a piece of work."

"Tell me about it. Beatrice said she burst into our studio, even. Can't you stop her from doing that?"

"I'll ask for an officer to be stationed at your door. But you might want to have someone drive you to your studio for the next coupla days so she doesn't ambush you in the parking lot. And screen all your calls."

"Will do." I nodded to a man who passed me on the path. Probably another vendor headed for the meeting, judging by a thick portfolio he carried under his arm. "Look, I've gotta go. I'm here for this big meeting of wedding planners. They're supposed to do a tribute to Charlotte this morning. I'll let you know how it goes."

"Roger that. And I'll keep you posted on the coroner's report. Take care."

I clicked off the line and returned the phone to my pocket. Unlike the stranger ahead of me, who swung his portfolio back and forth, I kept all my pictures on my phone. The stream of images showed my hats from every possible angle and in every possible light. I followed the man all the way to the mansion, where we climbed a marble staircase that brought visitors to a wide-plank porch.

The mansion's double-wide door stood open, and two very different women flanked its sides. On one side was the stranger I'd met in the registration cottage; the one who'd been so preoccupied with her precious committees. On the left stood Susannah Wan, the association's president, an older woman in an elegant Chanel suit the color of ripe cherries.

Susannah was a fixture on the Great River Road. Rumor had it Suzi, as she preferred to be called, single-handedly launched the wedding industry here when she planned the lavish nuptials for a former astronaut. Of course, that was twenty years ago, but people still gushed about the wedding as if it took place last week.

While she normally looked chic and youthful, today dark rings underscored Suzi's eyes and thick lines bracketed her mouth. She obviously hadn't slept well the night before, and the morning sun only exaggerated her condition.

I tried to catch her gaze as I moved over the threshold, but she abruptly turned away.

How odd. As a matter of fact, she wasn't the only person who wouldn't acknowledge me as I walked along. My favorite photographer hurried right past me, without so much as a hello. Then another business contact decided to study her shoes the minute I reached the porch. And finally, why did one of the most popular florists in town duck behind her assistant when she spied me? Was my imagination playing tricks on me, or were people avoiding me?

I stopped in the middle of the hall and whirled around. Did everyone know about the crime scene yesterday? That *my* hat stand was used to kill Charlotte Devereaux? If so, people sure had a strange way of showing it. Instead of coming right out and asking me about it, they'd rather pretend I didn't exist.

My shoulders sagged as realization dawned. Like it or not, there wasn't much I could do about it at the moment. So, I continued to walk to the restaurant, where the association normally held its monthly meetings, with my head down and my mood subdued.

The entire crowd seemed somber, unlike other months, when backslaps and chitchat and yoo-hoos filled the space. I followed the others into the room and headed for a table by a large picture window that overlooked the garden. Another lady approached the spot after me, but she abruptly turned away when she realized I'd be sitting at the table.

By the time Suzi stepped behind the podium and called the meeting to order, I had every seat to myself.

"I'd like to welcome y'all to our January meeting." Even with a microphone, Suzi's voice was soft. "I'm Suzi Wan, the president here. Now, I'm sure you've already heard about the terrible tragedy that happened yesterday with one of our members."

Something tickled my sleeve at that point, and I turned to see a heavyset man with a laptop plop down next to me. Obviously this newcomer didn't know—or care—about the role I played in Charlotte's murder. After a moment, the smell of cigar smoke reached me, no doubt imbedded in his checkered sport coat.

Meanwhile, Suzi struggled to compose herself. "For those of you who don't know, Charlotte Devereaux was a founding member of this association. I'm afraid—well . . . I'm afraid there's no good way to say this. She passed away yesterday."

Someone behind me gasped; probably a visitor who didn't have access to the local rumor mill. My tablemate reached for his dinner napkin, which he used to furiously fan his face.

I was about to lean over and suggest he might be more comfortable without the heavy sport coat when I noticed something on the coat's lapel. He'd pinned a name tag there, which had the flowery logo for Happily Ever After Events.

"Excuse me," I whispered. When he didn't react, I moved closer. "Excuse me. But are you Charlotte's cousin?"

Still nothing. Obviously, he was too overcome with grief to talk. Either that, or he was like everyone else in the room and chose to ignore me.

"Look, I'm sorry," I whispered. "But I don't know what happened yesterday at the Factory. I didn't have anything to do with it—you have to believe me."

The stranger remained silent, but his left eye twitched, which told me everything I needed to know.

Suzi continued to speak, but by now she looked miserable. "I know this has been hard for everyone. Charlotte was one of our best volunteers. She loved to greet people at things like this. I thought it'd be nice to hear a few words from her family, so I invited her cousin, Paxton Haney, to be with us today. Many of you know Paxton from the special-events company he ran with Charlotte. Please join me in welcoming him to the podium."

A polite smattering of applause sounded, and the man beside me rose. Once he lumbered onstage with the laptop, he finally remembered the napkin in his other hand, which he threw to the ground.

"Thank you," he said, upon reaching the podium and opening the computer. "As you can imagine, we're all still shocked about what happened yesterday. The family's trying to make sense of it all. There's so much we don't know. But, I do know Charlotte loved this group, and she loved all of you."

As if on cue, a black-vested waiter stepped forward from the sidelines. The moment he flicked a switch on the wall, a roller shade at the top of each window began to unfurl down the panes, bit by bit, accompanied by the soft whir of an electric motor. At the same time, another waiter unspooled a projector screen placed directly behind the podium.

Once in place, the white-woven screen provided the only light in the darkened room.

I blinked when a full-color image of Charlotte appeared on the screen.

"My cousin was a visionary," Paxton said. "Why, just this weekend, she told me all about her plans for our company. Said she let a few of you folks in on the news, and she wanted to make a big announcement next week." His voice caught. "Now she'll never get the chance. But you know our Charlie. Always reaching out for bigger and better."

A few heads nodded, a ripple of shadows that moved across the room.

"Y'all know what I'm talking about, right?" he said, suddenly reinvigorated. "Most people are happy to work their nine-to-five, but not Charlie. She wouldn't stop until she put Happily Ever After Events on the map. 'Course, she started in this business at a very young age."

He reached for the laptop again and tapped a button. Another image immediately appeared on the screen. There was Charlie, only several years younger, with a messy apron tied around her waist.

"Charlie began her career as a baker," he said. "Did y'all know that? She got up at four and started icing cupcakes at the crack of dawn." The laugh he gave sounded forced. "Good ones too. Always told me the only reason she didn't become a baker was because of the crazy hours. But she knew she wanted to add a bakery to our business, and now was the right time."

Another click on the laptop and a different image appeared. It was still Charlie in an apron, but a few wrinkles creased her eyes and the apron looked clean and pressed.

"'Course, this time Charlie planned to hire a baker for our business. She took this photo for our new advertising campaign. She wanted to include a flower shop, a photo studio, some musicians, and even a DJ service. It was 'all systems go' as far as Charlie was concerned." He paused, at last dropping the fake smile. "Now she'll never get a chance to see her dreams come true."

Someone began to whisper behind me, the noise like cannon fire in the quiet room. It set off a ripple of sound that swept over the restaurant. Pretty soon, Suzi resumed her place behind the podium and roughly reclaimed the microphone.

"Now, now." She waved her hand to silence the chattering crowd. "We're trying to remember Charlotte here. Please show some respect. You can talk among yourselves when we're done."

She nodded sternly at Paxton, who resumed his spot and once more tapped the laptop. This time a professional portrait of Charlotte appeared: a glossy black-and-white of her looking straight ahead.

"She took this picture only last week," he said. "It was for that ad campaign, but now we'll show it at her funeral. Which you're all invited to, of course. It'll be at the Rising Tide Baptist Church, right here in Riversbend. We'll start at four come Friday. Lights, please?"

The same waiter from before returned to the wall to call up the roller screens, while Paxton closed his laptop and stepped aside. Daylight flooded the room.

Once my eyes adjusted, I began to scan the crowd. I'd promised Lance a full report on the day's activities and I didn't want to disappoint him.

I glanced over to the head table first. The girl from the registration cottage was there, with her head bent over something or other in her lap. Every once in a while, her finger flicked up in a telltale motion, which meant she'd no doubt placed her cell phone there. She must be checking her Facebook or e-mail account, or maybe shopping on a website that sold shoes.

Meanwhile, Suzi dismissed the meeting by weakly thumping the gavel before she tottered off the stage. That left only Paxton and the girl with the cell phone there. Instead of heading for the exit, like most of the crowd, Charlotte's cousin scanned the room, until he caught my eye. He stared at me as he stepped off the stage and began to walk toward my table.

When he reached me, he glowered. "I didn't think you'd still be here. You have some nerve to show up like this."

"Excuse me?"

"You heard me. I almost said something earlier, but there were too many people around us. Don't you think you've done enough damage?"

I dropped my napkin to the ground, like he'd done, and rose. "I don't know what you're talking about, Mr. Haney. Look, I'm sorry about your cousin; I really am. But it's not fair to blame me for her death."

"My family told me your weapon was found by her body yesterday. How do you explain that?"

"It wasn't a weapon!" I didn't mean to yell, but I was sick of being doubted. "It was a hat stand. Someone took it from my studio."

"So you say. Just do my family a favor and stay away from the memorial service on Friday. Don't even think of going to it."

"B-b-b-u-u-t-t—" I sputtered. *How dare he tell me where I could and couldn't go!*

"But nothing. Stay away."

My mouth fell open as my mind whirled. While I wanted more than anything to "lay down the country," as my grandpa would say, and lay it down good, part of me understood Paxton's response.

For all this man knew, I had played a role in Charlotte's death. How would I feel if our roles were reversed? He obviously needed someone to blame, and I made an easy target. I might've done the very same thing if I stood in his shoes.

So, I swallowed my anger, although it left a bitter taste in my mouth. "If that's what you want, I won't go."

"It is." He began to walk away, taking with him the smell of burned tobacco.

Sweet mother of pearl. The day had just begun, and already I wanted to curl up under the table and take a good, long nap.

Chapter 5

By the time I left the meeting, even the girl checking her cell phone had vanished. Unfortunately, Paxton's scolding affected me more than I cared to admit, and I left in a daze, with no particular plan other than to arrive at my car at some point.

I longed to return to the Factory, where I could lick my wounds in private. As I made my way through the empty foyer, though, I gradually slowed. Hadn't I promised Vernice I'd visit her in the registration cottage? If I left the property now, she'd be disappointed, and I couldn't afford to lose another friend at this point.

Besides, a warm conversation with her might actually lift my spirits. Vernice wouldn't care about my role in Charlotte's murder, and she wouldn't pretend I didn't exist. It might be the perfect antidote to the cold shoulders I received everywhere else.

Renewed by the thought, I set off for the front door, which stood open. With nothing around me but yards of empty space and closed conference-room doors, I studied the ground as I walked, the soles of my shoes whooshing over the wool carpet.

I finally glanced up when I arrived at the exit. Two figures huddled on the steps outside, their heads bent together.

One of them, an older woman in a crisp blue-jean jacket and shiny ballerina bun, made tight gestures as she spoke. Her companion was at least three decades younger, and she wore a flowing skirt with combat boots.

I recognized both of them. Bettina Leblanc always wore her hair in a bun, even when she wasn't working as a baker in her shop. There was no mistaking the florist, either. Dana LeBoeuf, the woman behind Flowers by Dana, loved to shop for clothes in thrift stores, including her shoes.

They didn't notice me, so I quickly moved to the wall beside the doorframe and pressed my back against the cool surface. I definitely heard voices. Although part of me debated whether I should eavesdrop on a private conversation, another part didn't care, since Paxton's bullying left me feeling less than charitable.

"Of course, she knew." Bettina's voice quivered with rage. "Those additions would put the rest of us out of business. She *had* to know."

"We can't be sure." Unlike Bettina, Dana's tone remained calm. "Maybe she thought we'd all work together."

"Together? *Together?* How can you say that? The last thing this town needs is another baker. Or another florist."

"Now, calm down." Apparently, Dana refused to take the bait. "She never said she'd do flowers for weddings. Or cakes. Maybe she planned to do corporate events."

"Who do you think keeps us going during the off-season?" Bettina bit into the words. "We can't depend on the wedding business during wintertime. You know that."

"She's not even here to defend herself—"

"Wait a minute." Bettina quickly cut her off. "You knew, didn't you? That's it: You knew exactly what Charlotte was planning to do."

"I don't know what you're talking about."

"That's it! She told you. She went behind our backs and planned all this out, and then she told you about it."

Dana didn't respond. Just to be safe, I held my breath so neither would hear me.

"Well?" Bettina finally asked. "Aren't you going to say something?"

"Okay. You're right. She told me last week. She didn't want me to be surprised."

"So, why didn't you tell the rest of us? Maybe we could've done something."

"That's the point." Now Dana sounded angry. Although I couldn't see her, I imagined she'd planted her fists on her hips. "There was nothing anyone could do. She was determined to have her way."

"We could've tried. For all we know, her cousin will go through with her plans. Now that she's gone, maybe he'll take the ball and run with it."

"That's *not* going to happen."

A beat or two of silence, which meant it was time to hold my breath again.

"You don't know that." Bettina's voice dripped sarcasm. "No one can say for sure."

"I know . . . I took care of it, okay?"

"What do you mean, 'you took care of it'?"

"Just what I said. There's not going to be any expansion. You have to trust me on this."

At that moment, something vibrated in my pocket, like a bee trapped inside the lining. I rushed to grab the phone, but not quickly enough. The ringtone shattered the calm, so loudly that even I flinched.

There was no time to think. I spun around the doorframe, as if I happened upon the two women by accident. At the same time, I shoved my hand in my pocket and silenced the phone.

"Well, hello!" I tried to look surprised, which wasn't easy, considering they stood right in front of me.

"Missy?" Bettina said. "What're you doing here?"

"I forgot my phone in the restaurant." I waved vaguely behind me. "Silly me. I'd forget my head if it wasn't attached."

While Dana seemed to accept the explanation, Bettina looked skeptical.

"That so? We were just talking about things. This and that. Catch any of it?"

"Who, me?" I puffed out my cheeks. "Don't be silly. I've got a lot on my mind and my head's in the clouds most of the time these days."

"It's okay." Dana shot a quick look at Bettina. "We were finished anyway. And I've gotta get back to work."

"You and me both," I said. "That was some bombshell Paxton dropped on the crowd, wasn't it? That bit about Charlotte wanting to expand their business. I didn't see that one coming."

"*You* don't have anything to worry about." Bettina's tone was icy. "She didn't say anything about hats. Now I, on the other hand . . ."

"Bettina?" Dana threw her another look. "We can talk about it some other time. Missy and I both have to get back to work."

"Fine. Have it your way."

"Well, it was good to see you two." While I was still curious about their conversation, I didn't want Vernice to think I'd abandoned her. "I hope we run into each other again."

We parted ways on the steps, with Bettina and Dana heading east, toward the parking lot, while I aimed straight ahead, toward the registration cottage.

Such a strange conversation. What did Dana mean when she said she had "taken care of it"? She'd confused both me and Bettina. It sounded ominous, even coming from a flower child in combat boots who made wedding bouquets for a living.

I thought it over as I set off for the registration cottage, where I found Vernice. She and I chatted about this, that, and another thing until it was time to leave.

By the time I said good-bye, a topcoat of wet, dark clouds painted the sky. I quickly headed for Ringo and put up the soft top before starting the engine.

After exiting the parking lot and cruising onto the access road, I passed sugarcane fields and a smoking power plant. I barely noticed the pale smokestack, though, because my thoughts kept returning to the morning's strange turn of events. Along with the conversation between Bettina and Dana, there was the run-in with Paxton Haney. He'd stormed over to my table, eyes flashing, which made me thankful a few other people still milled around us.

At one point, Ringo bumped over a pothole in the road, and my memories vanished. Maybe my best option was to return to the hat studio. Stormie Lanai should be gone by now, and I could hole up in my workroom, which was the one place on earth I felt safe.

So I entered the on-ramp for Highway 18. The more I thought about the workroom, the more my hands relaxed on the steering wheel. After a while, I even imagined a piece of cool millinery wire under my thumb, instead of a nubby wheel cover. I had total control in that space, which was something I couldn't say about anywhere else at the moment.

After cruising along for several miles, deep in thought, I entered the off-ramp for Bleu Bayou and headed for the Factory. By the time I reached the parking lot, relieved to find a FedEx truck parked where the news van had been, a few raindrops splashed against the soft top.

I parked next to Ambrose's Audi and made a beeline for my studio. All of our shops came with a French door that opened onto the parking lot, to give customers easy access to our wares. Some of us also had a window, and I spied Beatrice through ours as I walked into the studio.

"Hey, there." She stood at the cash register with a notebook in front of her, which she slapped closed.

"Whew. What a morning." I walked to a bar stool by her and sat down.

"That bad?" Today Beatrice wore a different pair of chandelier earrings—emerald, this time—and one grazed her J. Crew sweater when she cocked her head at me.

"Worse. But at least I didn't see Stormie's news van outside. Please tell me she's gone."

"She is."

My eyes swept over the studio. *Everything looks the same.* Maybe I'd been paranoid about Stormie "borrowing" one of my hat stands for her news report, since nothing had been taken. My favorite display still perched by the front door, with a white top hat, fancy riding crop, and pair of exquisite leather boots. Ditto for a beaded fascinator I'd paired with some opera gloves near the cash register. Even the smallest display—a flower headband balanced on a bolt of Belgian lace—hadn't been touched. Maybe my imagination was working overtime. "Thank goodness for small miracles. How are things going here?"

For some reason, Beatrice wouldn't look at me.

"Beatrice?" She always acted this way when she had to deliver bad news. "Spill it. What's going on?"

"Why don't you tell me about the meeting first?" She quickly swept out from behind the counter and took the bar stool next to mine.

"*Okkkaaayyy.* But you're acting really weird." I tried to remember everything that took place before my run-in with Paxton Haney and before the conversation I overhead at the door to the mansion. "I'm sure you know by now who died. It was Charlotte Devereaux."

She nodded. "Yeah, I heard. It's all over town. I met her a couple of times in the atrium. She seemed like a real nice lady."

"She was. You should've seen the crowd that turned out for the meeting this morning. I think a lot of them already knew it was Charlotte. The strangest thing happened, though. I got the feeling people were avoiding me."

"Really? Why's that?"

"They kept their distance, for one thing, and then her cousin went off on me about the murder weapon. Do you think everyone knows the police found my hat stand at the crime scene?"

She swiveled her chair around. "I don't know. It's hard to say. Maybe."

I followed her lead and turned toward the counter too. "I don't *think* I was imagining it."

"But, maybe they were preoccupied. You know . . . just sad about Charlotte." She began to play with the notebook, running her thumb along its edge.

"Maybe. But even Bettina, the caterer, did it."

"Really? The owner of Pink Cake Boxes was there? I would've come if I'd known that."

"Yeah, but she acted strange, like everyone else. Just a second." I casually took the book away from Beatrice. It was the store's calendar. When I flipped it open, a series of angry red slashes appeared on the page. "Okay, Beatrice. What's going on?"

She finally dropped the act. "Um, I may have some bad news."

"Stop beating around the bush. What is this?"

"We had three cancellations today. Two from brand-new clients, and then that girl from Shreveport called."

I groaned. "Not Trudi Whidbee." The oil baron's daughter had commissioned a 5,000-dollar veil to match an equally expensive wedding gown. I'd already worked up a preliminary sketch for her. "What did she say?"

"She doesn't want it anymore. Apparently, Charlotte was her wedding planner. Said something about bad karma, I think."

"That's all?"

"Pretty much. The other two brides made up some lame excuses about not feeling well. Honestly, how could two people get strep throat on the same day?" She harrumphed. "The cowards."

I ran my hand along the page. Of course, everyone knew about the murder weapon. This was Bleu Bayou, after all, where news traveled faster than a bolt of lightning. At this rate, I'd be lucky to have *any* clients left by the end of the week. "What about tomorrow's appointments?"

When she didn't respond, I raised my hand. "That's okay. Don't say it. I'm guessing everyone canceled for tomorrow too."

I quickly calculated the loss. Five appointments . . . gone. Just like that. In the space of two days, I'd lost at least 10,000 dollars in revenue. I tried to ignore the zeros flashing before my eyes, but the numbers refused to fade.

"We're still okay, right?" Beatrice asked.

"Of course we're okay." There was no need to worry her. If Beatrice thought something was wrong with the studio, clients would sense it the minute they walked through the front door. "We're fine. Don't you worry a bit."

In all honesty, we were anything *but* fine. I needed those orders to make up for December, which was always sluggish. That was what happened every year, when January's receipts made up for the holiday's shortfall.

I quickly grabbed the calendar and slid off the bar stool. "Time to make some calls."

Since she still looked worried, I plastered a smile on my face. "Relax, Bea. We're not going anywhere. I just need to do damage control. Why don't you focus on inventory today? We're almost out of peach sinamay, and that ivory petersham is gone too. If anyone else calls and tries to cancel, say I'll call 'em back."

She finally nodded, so I began to take measured steps to the workroom. While I wanted to fall to the ground and throw a good old-fashioned hissy fit, that wouldn't do anyone a lick of good. Instead, I did what my grandma always said: I put on my big-girl panties and faced the music.

I softly closed the workroom door behind me. I longed to feel cool millinery wire under my thumb, like I'd imagined in the car. Since that wasn't going to happen, I laid the calendar on the drafting table and somberly took the chair beside it.

First things first. I pulled out my cell and eyed a phone number listed next to Trudi Whidbee's name in the calendar.

The phone rang at least four times before she picked up.

"Yes?" She sounded peeved.

"Hi, Trudi. It's me. Missy DuBois."

"I know who you are. I have caller ID. What can I do for you, Missy?"

The cool tone chilled me. "I think there's been a little . . . uh . . . misunderstanding."

"Is that so?"

"Yes. Beatrice told me you canceled your appointment for today."

"What could I do? The news is all over the television. That poor girl died right behind your studio. I don't think I could bring myself to go back there." She sighed dramatically. "You know, I only hired Charlotte because *you* recommended her."

"I thought I was doing you a favor."

"Hmmm. Some favor. Look, I don't want to be ugly, but I think it's best if we part ways. I'm sure you can understand. As a matter of fact—" she delicately cleared her throat "—there won't be a wedding, after all. So I definitely don't need your services."

I squinted at the phone in my hand. What did she mean, no wedding? "But—"

She hung up before I could finish. Of all the things I expected to hear, that wasn't one of them. I expected her to say she wanted a new wedding planner. That she was starting from scratch, milliner included, which left no room for me. Those things I could understand. But no wedding?

I eyed the other red slashes on the calendar. After my stilted conversation with Trudi, it was anyone's guess how the remaining calls would go.

Chapter 6

After calmly explaining the situation to the other brides who'd canceled—which wasn't easy, since I longed to wail about the unfairness of it all—I finally lowered the phone, utterly exhausted. Turned out Beatrice was right about the girls using strep throat as an excuse. By the end of our calls, the second bride agreed to come in at three, while the other one would come in at four.

Now I needed to plot out my strategy for the first appointment. To begin with, I'd greet the client at the front door and give her a grand tour of the studio to convince her nothing was wrong. Then I'd tell her all about my alibi for yesterday's murder. I could even throw in a 10-percent discount on her order, which would seal the deal.

I slumped against the chair wearily and eyed a clock on the wall. *Gracious light.* It was already two. Even though the wedding planners' meeting included a light breakfast, I'd been too preoccupied to eat anything, and now my stomach rumbled. At this rate, Beatrice would find me in a puddle on the floor if I didn't get some nourishment.

I grabbed my cell and strode out of the workroom. "Boy, am I glad that's over." My stomach angrily complained as I met Beatrice by the counter.

"How'd it go?" She'd been rifling through our Rolodex, no doubt searching for the phone numbers of our fabric suppliers.

"Not bad. I saved our three o'clock and four o'clock appointments. I'm going to give each of them a ten-percent discount, so don't let me forget that."

"Will do." She brushed a snatch of peach straw from her sweater. "What about Trudi?"

"No dice. Did know she canceled her wedding?"

Beatrice's eyes widened. "You're kidding! That's news to me. What kind of fool ditches Trudi Whidbee and all that cash?"

"For all you know, she ditched him." My belly complained again, and this time in no uncertain terms. "Listen, I haven't had a thing to eat all day and I'm starving. I'm going to grab a *kolache* at Grady's place. Do you want anything?"

When she shook her head, the earrings swung back and forth like pendulums. "No thanks. I'll stay here. I'm done with the inventory on the sinamay, and I was about to call in our order. Want me to get some cream straw too, while I'm at it?"

"No, we'd better not. Let's try to watch our expenses until we get some billings. How much straw do we have left?"

"About a roll and a half of the basket-weave and a little less of cobweb."

"That should do it for a while. Thanks for asking, though, and I'll see you in a bit." I walked across the studio, to the exit. As I shut the door behind me, I instinctively glanced at the studio next to mine. Since Ambrose and I shared a wall, it was easy to check in with him from time to time. Especially since he often forgot to eat lunch too, which made him cranky by the end of the day.

I glanced through the window to his studio and spotted him near the three-way mirror. A gorgeous brunette stood on a pedestal in front of him. She had porcelain skin, auburn hair—like mine—and an impossibly tiny waist.

When she twirled, the ball-gown skirt around her twinkled like a starburst.

I forgot about my hunger for a moment. Even though he was with a client, I should have probably checked on Ambrose . . . for his own well-being, of course. After working up a respectable smile, I entered the room and approached the duo.

Ambrose didn't even notice me. He continued to study the girl as she turned, the crystals swirling like a meteor shower.

"Uh, Ambrose?"

The client stopped mid-twirl. "He's busy right now," she told my reflection.

"I can see that."

Finally, Ambrose glanced up. "Hi, Missy. Got my hands full here."

"That's okay. I don't want to bother you. You go right ahead."

He was supposed to catch my drift and pause. When he didn't, I cleared my throat and tried again. "I just want to know if I can pick you up some lunch. I'm going to Grady's and I thought—well, I thought . . ."

Was that a scowl? I was so taken aback by his expression, my smile froze.

"Uh, only if you want me to get you something, that is."

"You *don't* have to do that." The sour expression remained as he studied the ball-gown skirt. "This could take a while."

The girl on the pedestal decided to chime in. "I'd listen to him, if I were you."

Instead of scowling at her too, Ambrose actually smiled. "I'll be fine. I'm not even hungry right now."

I inched forward. "But I really don't mind getting you something. I was kinda hoping we could eat it together. When you're through here, that is."

Evidently, the client didn't like my idea. "He said he's not hungry. And he's right in the middle of something. So it looks like you wasted your time coming over here."

"I heard what he said, thank you." I willed Ambrose to back me up. I had a million things I wanted to tell him, but how could I, when he wouldn't give me the time of day? *Darn him and his obsessive attention to detail.* Not to mention, I felt my old insecurities bubble up whenever he turned his back on me like that.

It happened every time he ignored me, which wasn't often. I immediately regressed to my childhood, to the little girl who lost both parents in a car accident. The smallest slight triggered the feeling that maybe I wasn't worth his attention after all. My own parents left me, so why shouldn't he? It was irrational, of course, but that didn't stop it from happening. The ghost of my childhood followed me around like a second shadow and resurfaced at the most inopportune times.

"Fine," I said. "I guess I'll see you later."

"Whatever." His gaze remained glued to that damn skirt. "See you later."

Men can be so clueless. I forced myself to retreat from the mirror. Going against every instinct, I somehow managed to walk to the French door and step over the threshold. Of all the times for him to ignore me, why did it have to be today? We had so much to discuss, but he acted like I was a nuisance. Which wasn't like him; and that was what bothered me most of all.

I frowned all the way to my car. After pausing in front of Ambrose's Audi first, where I gave his front tire a good, swift kick, I hopped into Ringo and fired up the engine. *Fine. Let him starve.* I'd scarf down two giant beignets, just to spite him.

Once out of the parking lot, I turned onto the feeder road and the Factory's roofline soon disappeared from view. Instead, the watery stretch of pavement that lead to downtown Bleu Bayou appeared in the windshield.

Before long, I reached Grady's doughnut shop. Even with scattered clouds to block the sunshine, the neon arrow on its roof still glowed in all its kitschy glory.

Some people urged Grady to keep the sign and the 1950s décor when he bought the place. Others advised him to do a total makeover. Fortunately, he listened to the first group, and the sign, red-leather banquette seats, bubblegum-pink straw dispensers, and checkerboard floor tiles remained.

I pulled into the shop's parking lot, which was almost empty. Then I hurried through the plate-glass door, where I spied Grady at his usual spot behind the counter.

Today he wore a white T-shirt, faded jeans, and a tie-dye do-rag over his blond curls. "Hey, there!" His voice was warm and welcoming.

I swerved dramatically as I approached the counter, clutching my stomach for good measure. "Help. Need beignet. Can't . . . last . . . much . . . longer."

"Bravo." He straightened and clapped a few times before snatching an oiled paper sack from a pile in front of him. "Would you like to eat it here, Miss Streep, or will you take it to go?"

"Guess I'll eat it here. Looks like you have a few open tables." I nodded at the lone diner—an old man in the corner—surrounded by empty booths.

"Hey . . . it's usually busy all morning. This is my slow time." The top of the do-rag showed when Grady bent to retrieve a beignet from the case.

"I know that. I'm just messin' with you."

He reached a bit farther, and a sliver of tattoo peeked out from under his sleeve. It was a giant whisk on his right bicep. The tattoo always fascinated me, since I expected someone like Grady to choose a skull and crossbones, dagger, or maybe a lion for a tattoo. Not something as conservative as a whisk, his occupation notwithstanding.

Once Grady straightened, he dropped two beignets in the sack, not one, and the tattoo disappeared. "Coffee to go with it?" He nodded to a Bunn machine behind him.

"Sure. Why not."

He pushed aside a newspaper he'd propped against a display case to make room for the beignets on the counter. We both noticed the headline on the paper's front page at the same time.

"Ouch." He sucked in his cheeks. "You weren't supposed to see that."

It was the front section of the *Bleu Bayou Impartial Reporter.* Under the banner lay the words *murder, wedding planner,* and *bystander,* all in twenty-point type.

"Have you read the story yet?" he asked.

"No. I was busy this morning. I'm not surprised it's in the newspaper already, though."

"Want to talk about it?"

"I'd love to."

"Let me grab you some coffee first." He turned to the machine and pulled a carafe from its burner. After scrutinizing the dark sludge, he quickly took a whiff and put it back. "That stuff's not fit for human consumption. I'll make you some fresh."

"No, that's okay." I plucked up the sack of beignets. "Don't bother. I really came in for some food and conversation. How much do I owe you?"

"It's on the house." He winked and stepped out from behind the counter. Before joining me, he whisked off the do-rag and tossed it aside, which caused a curl to spring forward on his cheek. "Come on. I have just the spot."

He headed for a booth placed catercorner to the front door, no doubt to keep the cash register in sight.

"Perfect." I slid into the booth with him. Although I didn't want to be rude, enough was enough already, so I grabbed a beignet and took a hearty bite. Warm dough filled my mouth, the fatty taste of the cooking oil offset by sweet, powdered sugar. A smattering of crystals sprinkled to the table like fresh snow.

He grinned. "Now there's a gal who likes her beignets."

I barely heard him as I launched into another bite. After several blissful seconds, I finally came up for air. "These are awesome, Grady."

"Thanks. My mee-maw taught me how to bake. It's all about getting the oil just right. Most folks don't take time to let it cook all the way. So . . . what's all this I've been reading about?"

I reluctantly put the half-eaten beignet down and wiped my fingers on a napkin. "I'm sure it's all there in the newspaper."

"Yeah, they said something about finding Charlotte behind your store."

"It's worse than that. *I* was the one who found her. After I called the police, I had to go to headquarters to give them my statement."

His eyes narrowed. "I'm sorry you had to do that. It must've been awful."

"Thanks. I'm sorry too. The good news is my friend is a detective, and he'll get a coroner's report on it sometime tonight. We're hoping it gives a clue about who did it."

"I know your friend. He's the one I met last summer."

To be honest, I'd completely forgotten about that. It must have happened during Mellette Babineaux's investigation, when Lance took over the case. He and I met at Dippin' Donuts every so often to go over our notes. Those meetings seemed like a million years ago by now. "I forgot about that. Say, Grady. Can I ask you a question?"

"Anything." He looked at me so intently, I had to glance away. Were his eyes always so blue, or did I notice them today because we sat side by side?

"I don't know why these things keep happening to me. I mean, it's not like I go around looking for trouble. It kinda finds me on its own." Finally, I glanced at him again.

Flecks of gold floated through the rims of his irises. "Maybe it's like that saying . . . when bad things happen to good people. Sounds to me like you're going through a rough patch."

"But it's not the first time. Why do I keep finding dead bodies? I mean . . . who gets wrapped up in three murder investigations in two years? It's not normal, and I wish it would stop."

"Yeah, but I think you can handle it." He appraised me with those beautiful eyes. "You're a lot stronger than you think. Stronger than most people around here, I'd say."

"I don't know, Grady. This time it could shutter my business. I had three brides cancel on me today. Three! Who knows how the rest of the week will go?"

"I know something that might cheer you up." He took a deep

breath and then slowly exhaled. "I've been meaning to ask you something for a while. Here goes. Will you go out to dinner with me?"

I blinked. "Uh, come again?"

Fortunately, he didn't seem to take offense. "It's a simple question, really. Would you go on a date with me?"

While I've never been at a loss for words, for some reason I couldn't get my tongue to work. Try as I might, the words stalled at the back of my throat.

"Guess I'll take your silence as a compliment," he said. "You never expected a great catch like me to ask you that. I understand."

Finally, I woke up. Truth be told, the man sitting beside me was worlds, if not solar systems, apart from me. His world was black leather, tie-dyed do-rags and heavy metal, while I favored Lilly Pulitzer shifts, delicate hats, and Harry Connick, Jr. CDs. He was handsome, but I'd never once considered him a dating prospect. "Well, uh . . ."

"Do you want some time to think about?"

Then again, what is there to think about? Ambrose had blown me off in front of a stranger not more than ten minutes before. After spending a year and a half with that man, what did I have to show for it? One measly date—although it *was* an incredible date—and sleepless nights spent wondering whether he would ask me out again. Time was definitely not on my side when it came to Ambrose Jackson. "I don't have to think about it, Grady. Sure, I'll go out with you."

"Oh. Okay, then. That's great. Really, really great." He beamed like a cat that had swallowed a canary, as my grandpa would say.

I awkwardly rose from the booth and plucked the doughnut sack from the table. "Why don't you call me? I should probably get back to work now. Don't want my assistant to think I'm playing hooky from the shop."

"How does tomorrow night sound? And maybe you should wear that red sweater with the black sleeves. It's one of my favorites."

I hesitated. "*Oookkkkaaayyy.*" No one had ever asked me to wear a certain outfit on a date before. *Wonder what that means?* "Guess I'll talk to you tomorrow, then." I fiddled with the doughnut sack, searching for a diversion. "I still owe you for lunch, by the way."

"I told you . . . it's on the house." He braced his palms against the table and rose. Out peeked the tattoo again, looking as adorable as ever.

What have I gotten myself into? Grady was Lynyrd Skynyrd, muscled biceps, and a slick Ford Mustang with aluminum wheels. It would never work . . . or would it?

I waved good-bye and made a beeline for the front door. Once outside and safely behind the wheel of my convertible, I didn't bother to pop in the Harry Connick, Jr. CD. Somehow, it didn't feel right. And somehow, I couldn't get the sound of Ambrose's voice out of my head.

Chapter 7

As I drove away from the doughnut store, I mulled over my conversation with Grady and the earlier slight from Ambrose. The two men couldn't be more different.

On the one hand, Ambrose was sleek and stylish, like his black Audi Quattro. I also knew what to expect with him, since I'd lived with him for a year and a half.

Grady, on the other hand, was an unknown. He was rough-and-tumble, but soft enough to tattoo a whisk on his bicep. Not to mention those cornflower-blue eyes, which caught me off guard every time I stared at them.

Halfway through my reverie, the tip of the Factory's glass pyramid appeared on the horizon, which meant work was a few miles away. While most days I appreciated the short commute from one place to another, sometimes I longed for a real car ride, where I could drive and ponder and get lost in the silence.

In another minute or so, I arrived at the building's parking lot and pulled into the space next to Ambrose's car, which still sat vacant. I was more confused than ever by the time I arrived at the door to Crowning Glory.

"Hey, there." Beatrice stood beside our cash register with a half-eaten piece of cake in her hand. "You've been gone for a while, so I hit up Pink Cake Boxes for a sample. Is everything okay?"

"Am I that obvious?" I maneuvered around the display table near the door and met up with her by the counter.

A smudge of lemon painted her lower lip. "I know you. Something happened. You told me you were just grabbing lunch at the doughnut shop." She popped the last bit of cake into her mouth.

"Turns out, I got a whole lot more than I bargained for."

"I knew it! So, tell me everything." She scooted out from behind the counter and fell onto a bar stool. "What happened?"

"Well, you know Grady, right?" I slid onto the stool next to hers.

"Of course I do. Everyone does. I always thought he was kinda cute."

"Really? You never told me that before."

"That's because he's *waaayyy* too old for me. He must be . . . what, at least thirty?"

I rolled my eyes. "You're right . . . he's practically dead."

"You know what I mean. What happened with him?"

I paused. While I trusted Beatrice, she still worked for me, so I couldn't be too chatty. "Let's just say I think we're going on a date tomorrow night."

"Shut up!" It took a moment and then she clamped her hand over her mouth. "Sorry 'bout that." She spoke around her splayed fingers. "You just surprised me. Did he really ask you out?" Slowly, she pulled her hand away from her lips.

"Yep. We're going out to dinner tomorrow night."

"What about Ambrose? Does he know?"

"There's the problem. He *doesn't* know. And I'm not sure I want to tell him."

"No one said you have to tell him."

"I know, but I can't lie to him. What am I supposed to say when he asks where I'm going? We live in the same house, remember?"

"Maybe you could tell him you're having dinner with a friend. It's the truth. He doesn't have to know *which* friend."

I pondered that for a second. Technically, she was right. But she also was in her twenties, when people tended to act first and think later. I, however, knew exactly what the consequences of our date could be.

Since everyone in Bleu Bayou knew everyone else, I'd have no privacy during the evening. We always could have dinner in another town, but that was up to Grady, since *he'd* asked me out. "I don't know, Bea. It feels kinda sneaky. I'll have to think about it."

Thankfully, someone walked through the front door just then, which effectively ended our conversation. It was a heavyset girl in a floor-length denim skirt, who meekly entered the room.

I jumped up to greet her. "You must be my bride. Rebekkah, right?"

She nodded shyly, which bobbed the wheat-colored braid on her shoulder. "Yes, ma'am. Are you ready for me?"

"Of course. Right this way." I gently took her elbow and guided her to the counter. "This is my assistant, Beatrice. You'll see her sometimes when you come in for your fittings."

"Hi, there," Beatrice said. "Nice to meet you."

The girl nodded again. In addition to the denim skirt, she wore a black turtleneck and not a speck of makeup. This one might prove challenging.

When she finally spoke, she sounded apologetic. "I'm so sorry about canceling on you before. It's just that I heard so many rumors, I didn't know what to believe."

"That's okay. I understand. I'm just glad you changed your mind. C'mon, let's go back to the display area."

I took her other arm this time and carefully led her to a sitting area I'd created in the middle of the room. A pair of white-linen couches perched on a thick sheepskin rug, and a crystal chandelier hung over our heads. My goal was to create a modern, romantic space in the middle of a rustic, wood-paneled room, and I liked to think I pulled it off.

"Now . . . do you have a particular style in mind?" I eased her onto the couch.

"No, not really. I never really thought about it. The appointment was my mom's idea. She wanted to come with me today, but our dog got loose."

Praise the Lord for small favors. Usually, it's not a bride who gives me conniptions . . . it's her mother. For some reason, a lot of mothers think I can read their minds and create wonderful designs from the get-go. While it does happen, more often than not, the process involves give-and-take, floor samples, and reams of sketch paper.

Of course, I could understand why a mother might feel that way, since my designs cost hundreds—if not thousands—of dollars. "So, where are you going to have your wedding?" I asked.

"At Rising Tide Baptist Church. Both the ceremony and reception. You know, in the social hall."

That makes sense. This girl didn't seem the type to go for a gimmicky, turn-of-the century wedding on a local riverboat, complete with picture hats and parasols, or a sleek cocktail reception in the golden ballroom at Morningside Plantation. "Did you bring a picture of your gown?"

"Yes. Just like you asked." She opened a fringed leather purse and pulled out a clip from *Modern Bride*, which she handed over. The ad had been folded and refolded so many times, it felt like rice paper in my hand.

"The dress is lovely!"

She'd picked a wonderful design for her shape and size. A lace halter-top sprinkled with seed pearls flowed to a classic empire waist. "Let's see . . ." I stepped across the room to a side table. My old standby, a cathedral-length veil, complemented almost any gown, and even the pickiest mother could appreciate its conservative lines.

Then again . . . life was too short to always play it safe. I decided to roll the dice and headed for a different veil I'd pinned to the wall.

"I think we should start with this one." I removed some pushpins and walked to the three-way mirror with the veil. "Can you come here, please?" I flashed my most reassuring smile. "Trust me. I think you're going to love this."

The girl tentatively rose and approached the mirror, which she refused to look at.

"You don't like mirrors much, do you?" I asked.

"No, ma'am. I don't. Daddy always said it's better to have something to do than something to look at."

"Interesting. That may be, but I need to know what you think of this style." I whisked the veil from behind my back and carefully set it on her head. The fabric gently pillowed around her face like a puff of clouds.

She couldn't resist taking a quick peek at her reflection. Pops of light twinkled from the pearl comb I'd set at the crown, and layers of tulle tumbled to her shoulders. The volume from the multiple layers offset her round face beautifully.

"You look like an angel," I said.

Her breath caught in her throat. "I do, don't I?"

No matter what this girl's daddy told her about vanity, every girl deserved to feel beautiful on her wedding day. So, I made a big fuss over fluffing up the tulle and straightening the comb just so.

"I think we should definitely consider this one," I said. "It's called a bubble veil, and it'll highlight your neckline too."

She turned slightly. "Maybe this one wouldn't be so bad. Do lots of girls wear this style?"

"Some. It's designed to flatter a halter, like the one you've picked." I carefully studied the picture again. Although we'd found a winner, it wouldn't hurt to have a second, and more conservative, option. It might make the mother feel better about spending so much money on a custom veil if I provided more than one design. "You know, I also have a design for a more traditional, cathedral-length veil."

In fact, I should've thought of it sooner. Ever since Trudi Whidbee announced the end of her wedding, I'd been wondering what to do with the sketch of her veil. Of course, she'd had a five thousand dollar budget, which meant oodles of expensive Swarovski crystals and panels of Alençon lace. But, nothing said I couldn't simplify the design.

"That sounds pretty," she said. "But I do love this one."

"Just a second. Let me grab my sketch pad." I left the veil on Rebekkah's head, since she seemed so enamored by it, and then dashed to my workroom. Once there, I grabbed the sketch pad and returned to the mirror before she even finished a second turn.

"Now, it's a preliminary drawing, mind you." I showed her the sketch, which featured a flowing train with two tiers of lace and tulle. "I made this for another bride, but her wedding got canceled."

Rebekkah immediately blanched. "I'm sure it's nice and all, but I never could afford it."

"What makes you say that?" She hadn't given me much of a chance to describe it.

"That was for Trudi Whidbee's wedding, wasn't it? Everyone knows she canceled hers."

"You're right." Only then did I notice Trudi's name in the lower right-hand corner. "Of course, I could always change-up the design for you. We don't have to use this exact drawing."

"Well, it *is* beautiful." She eyed the sketch pad longingly. "But I don't know. That was supposed to be this super-expensive wedding, and I'm only having family and friends in the church social hall."

"Like I said, we can always change it up a bit. Instead of expensive crystals along the edge, we could use rhinestones, which don't cost nearly as much. And those extra lace inserts could go too."

She didn't seem convinced, though. "It's not just that. I heard about how her fiancé treated her. I don't want that kind of bad karma at my wedding."

"Well, it's totally up to you." I tapped the pad lightly against my thigh. "You're the client. Why don't we take a picture of you in the bubble veil instead and you can show it to your mom. I'll pull out a few more styles too."

"Thank you for understanding. And I'm hoping my mama can come with me to the next appointment. She has lots of ideas about what I should wear."

No doubt. I plastered a smile on my face and gently removed the veil from Rebekkah's head. "Like I always say: the more, the merrier."

Chapter 8

After taking Rebekkah's picture from every possible angle with her cell phone, it was time to wrap up the appointment.

I sent her away with a memory card full of photos in her phone and my sworn promise to give her a preliminary sketch by the end of the month. As the door gently closed, I began to compile a to-do list of all the supplies I'd need to order, including a hair-comb inset with faux Tahitian pearls, several yards of silk tulle, and a passel of inexpensive sequins for the edges.

The list was almost complete in my mind when I paused by the store's cash register, where Beatrice had propped open a section of newspaper, just like Grady had done.

"Sounds like your appointment went well," she said, without glancing up.

"Yeah, it did." I slid onto the bar stool and watched her peruse the front page of the *Bleu Bayou Impartial Reporter*. "Have you read the story about Charlotte yet?"

She nodded slightly. "Uh-huh. I'm just finishing it now."

"I saw it over at Grady's place. Boy, those reporters work fast."

"Guess they have to." She finished reading the article, and then she straightened. "It's crazy how they can write a whole story with only a little bit of information. I didn't know Charlotte Devereaux was born here."

"Yep. That's what makes it even sadder. A lot of people in Bleu Bayou knew her."

"Well, I didn't. Not really. We ran into each other a few times in the lobby, but mostly we talked about small stuff. Like the time the vending machine ate my quarter. She gave me another one that morning. That kind of thing."

"Too bad you never got to work with her. Lots of wedding planners are hyperactive—they have to be—but not Charlotte. She was so laid-back."

"I get that. And the reporter quoted that detective you know for the story."

"You mean Lance? You've met him before. He worked on Trinity Solomon's murder case, over at Morningside. I wonder what's up with him? We haven't spoken since this morning."

Truth be told, I'd been a bit distracted since our last phone call. Especially after my visits with Ambrose, Grady, and Rebekkah. "I think I'll call him. Our next appointment won't be here for a few minutes. You can find me in the workroom if you need me."

I brought the sketch pad with me as I made my way through the studio. Once I reached the back room, I tossed the pad on the drafting board and pulled out my cell. Since I'd added him to my speed dial, I simply tapped the screen and waited for him to answer.

"Hey, Missy. How's your day going?"

"So-so." His voice jostled a memory, but not quite hard enough for it to be clear. "I was supposed to call you, wasn't I?"

He chuckled. "Yeah, you were. You're becoming as forgetful as I am. How did the meeting go this morning?"

"That was it. I promised to tell you what I saw at the wedding planners' meeting."

After filling Lance in on everything that happened, I finally took a breath. "That's why I think Paxton Haney might've had something to do with Charlotte's death. He was *sooo* nervous. And it wasn't because he had to give a speech, either."

"You may have something there. Now that I've got the autopsy report, I think I'll pay him a visit this afternoon and ask him some questions."

My ears pricked up. "Really? You got the autopsy report back already?"

"Yeah, they rushed it for me. The ME's a personal friend."

"That's great." A strange sense of déjà vu washed over me as I slowly sank onto the chair behind the drafting table. "So, here we go again. Are you gonna tell me what's in that report, or do I have to beg you for it?"

"What do you mean?"

I delicately cleared my throat. "As you'll recall, I was the one who figured out who killed Mellette Babineaux. But it happened only after you finally showed me the autopsy report."

"You're right." He paused for a moment. "I couldn't have closed that case without you. You seem to have this freaky sixth sense when it comes to people who are lying. I used to hate that about you when we were kids. Remember the time I smashed my mom's picture frame on the tile?"

I chuckled. "How could I forget? You gashed your thumb, but you lied and said it was a paper cut from playing cards with me. Everyone knows you don't play slapjack with your thumbs, Lance."

"Yeah, but did you have to tell my mom that? Okay, here's the deal: I'll give you some of the highlights from the report, but you have to keep it quiet."

"Scout's honor. What did the ME find?"

Papers rustled over the line. "He wrote *unremarkable* by most of it. The final diagnosis was acute blunt-force trauma." Lance's voice fell flat as he began to read. "Multiple cranial penetrations to the back of the head, concentrated above the left earlobe."

I pictured Charlotte lying sideways in a whiskey barrel, with only the top of her head visible. The blood clotting her hair was burgundy, wasn't it?

He continued: "More of the same all the way through. Linear fracture on the left side of her skull, lacerations on the right cheek. Must've been from where she fell. Sure you want to hear the rest?"

"I do." I nodded eagerly, even though he couldn't see me.

"She had some contusions on her right forearm and wrist too, according to the report. The tox study showed a blood ethanol of point-oh-six. Probably had a few drinks before she was killed. Not bad, considering it was New Year's Eve and all."

"Amazing, really. Do you think she was working that night?"

"Could be. That might explain the low ethanol levels."

I leaned back in my chair. "Anything else?"

"Nothing much. The internal exam showed everything else was normal. Wait a second. This is the part I meant to talk to you about." He paused, and the rustling stopped. "Did you know at one point she'd had a kid?"

"A what?"

"A kid. During the internal autopsy, the ME found evidence of childbirth in her uterus."

I softly whistled. "Whoa. She never mentioned it. We weren't best friends or anything, but you'd think she would've said something. Not right away, maybe . . . but we worked together sometimes."

"Interesting. Well, the rest of the report is pretty routine. I'm going to make some calls, and then I think I'll head out to the Factory and interview her cousin."

"His office is close to mine. Do you mind if I tag along?"

"I dunno." The line fell silent. After a moment, he returned. "Okay, here's the deal. I'll let you listen in, but only because you solved those other cases. You have to let me do all the talking. You'll be there to observe, and maybe use that freaky sixth-sense thing you have."

"Deal. I won't say a word."

"Let's meet at five."

I didn't hesitate. "Sounds good. She would've done the same for me. There's no way I can sit by and let someone get away with killing her."

"I'll stop by your studio first, and then we can go together."

"No, that's okay. I'd rather meet you there. I talked two of my appointments out of canceling on me, and the last one won't be here until four. His office is right upstairs, so I could be there by five."

"Suit yourself. I'll see you in a bit. And I'm glad your clients didn't cancel. There's no reason for your business to suffer. You weren't even there that morning. Unless . . ." His voice suddenly trailed off.

"Unless what?" The silence unnerved me, since he'd obviously changed his mind about something. "What were you gonna say?"

"That maybe someone knew what they were doing when they committed the murder behind your studio. Maybe someone's trying to ruin your business."

The hairs on the back of my neck bristled. "There's no way! I don't believe it. That's crazy."

"We're talking about a murderer, Missy. They're not known for being sane."

It took me a while to absorb his words. I couldn't quite scoff, since it sounded almost crazy enough to be true.

"You still there?" He sounded worried.

"Yeah. I was thinking about what you said." I swiveled around until I spied a clock over the door. My next appointment would arrive in a few minutes. How could I greet her with a big smile, as if nothing was wrong? "Oh my gosh. What if you're right? What if someone's trying to ruin me?"

"It could be. The location . . . the murder weapon . . . even the person who found the body. Everything points to you. That doesn't sound like a coincidence. Have you pissed off anyone lately?"

"No. Well, maybe. I don't know. No one off the top of my head. I'll have to think about it."

"You do that. Maybe there's someone in your past, or someone who doesn't like you now. Either way, it sounds like you've made an enemy. Let's talk more about it when we meet up at five."

I mumbled good-bye and let the cell slide to my lap. What if Lance was right? What if someone was trying to ruin my business? Already three people had called to cancel their appointments, and who knew what tomorrow would bring?

Chapter 9

By the time I finished with the last appointment of the day, my cheeks ached from smiling so much. I whisked open the front door for the bride, still grinning, and then firmly shut it behind her.

Beatrice stood on a ladder across the way.

"Hallelujah, we're done," I said. "I thought that last appointment would never end. Are you happy it's over too?"

She'd jammed a handful of pushpins in her mouth, which she was using to reattach a veil to the wall. "Mmmppphhhh."

"I'll take that as a yes." I whisked out my cell and checked the clock on its screen. I had plenty of time before my meeting with Lance. Fortunately, my last appointment had brought her gown with her, which always sped things up, since I could match the headpiece exactly to her style. Most clients don't have that option, since most of them don't have time between dress fittings to schlep a gown all the way to my studio. This bride was different, though.

"Do you know that girl bought her wedding dress when she was only seventeen?" I asked. "Talk about planning ahead." I tsked all the way to the counter. "Look, I'm wiped out. Can you please close up the shop tonight? I'm supposed to meet someone upstairs."

Beatrice mumbled something that sounded exactly like her first response.

"Great. Thank you."

I grabbed my keys and turned to leave, but not before I spied my reflection in the three-way mirror. *Ugh.* The day had not been kind to my hair and makeup.

Only seven hours earlier, I'd whipped my hair into a French knot before the wedding planners' meeting. Now strands of hair straggled over my shoulders like leftover bits from a housekeeper's mop. Not to mention black mascara smudged the skin under my eyes. I looked like something a hound dog would drag under the porch, as Grandpa would say.

While I had a few minutes to spare, it wasn't enough time for a full makeover. I quickly rubbed at the mascara with my thumb, and then I snapped off the ponytail holder. Once I ran my fingers through my hair, I gathered everything back up again. *Voilà!* At least my hair and makeup looked respectable now.

"See you later, Bea. I'm heading upstairs. Have a good night."

She waved as I stepped through the exit. By now, the sky over the parking lot had pinked, and twilight cast streaks of gold and rose onto the clouds. There was no sign of rain, although a patchwork of puddles remained on the asphalt.

I began to pick my way to the atrium, momentarily distracted by a light that glowed in Ambrose's studio. *I shouldn't stop in, should I?* Normally, I wouldn't hesitate, but the memory of our earlier conversation loomed large in my mind.

So I blazed past with my head down, and I didn't stop walking until I reached the atrium. A bright light glowed inside it too, but the space was empty. Two sleek Mies van der Rohe couches and a pair of matching armchairs occupied the open, airy space, but nothing else. Even the elevator was empty, so I moved to the car and rode alone to the second floor, where the door whooshed open to expose a long hallway.

Framed artwork paraded along each side of the hall. Instead of oil paintings, though, the frames held colorful produce labels that paid homage to the building's past. The labels featured beautiful red peppers with curly green stems, artfully shaded burlap bags overflowing with seeds, and even an apple-cheeked sun or two.

At one point, I'd been told, factory workers shipped peppers from Bleu Bayou to Mexico, where another crew took out the seeds, ground them to a pulp, and then returned them. Most of the labels fell off the crates during the ride back home, but somehow these stickers survived.

The colorful artwork ended with a smiling sun. Next to it were the offices for Happily Ever After Events and, across the way, the bakery called Pink Cake Boxes.

A rectangle of light warmed the carpet in front of the custom-cake business, which didn't surprise me, since Bettina never seemed to leave the building. She parked her car in the last row of our parking lot and left it there until nightfall. Of course, her hard work paid off in spades and now she had a client list in the hundreds, not to mention a waiting list that stretched to three weeks during the wedding season.

I paused at the end of the hall. Come to think of it, maybe the wedding planners' meeting didn't make sense. Why would Charlotte want to add a bakery to their business? Bettina's shop lay right across the hall, and she'd already been crowned the best baker on the Great River Road. It didn't add up, and it obviously bothered Bettina, judging by her earlier conversation at the plantation.

No use to worry about it, though, with so many other things going on. I turned my back on the bakery and approached the door for Happily Ever After Events. Unlike the modern lobby downstairs—which was all straight lines, sleek furniture, and cool glass—someone had turned the wall here into a page from a Brothers Grimm fairy tale. Painted limestones with rounded corners framed an etched Dutch door, which stood half open. A faux stained-glass window perched next to it and, higher still, a rosebush bloomed over the doorframe. One of the tendrils even reached for the ceiling before it faded away in a green curlicue. I glanced down again when a voice sounded on the other side of the door.

"I'm not accusing you of anything." It was Lance, his words as sharp as a thorn painted on the rosebush. "You need to calm down."

My hand stalled over the doorknob.

"Do you have a warrant?" Now it was Paxton's turn, and he growled the words. "I'm pretty sure you need a warrant to come in here."

Quietly, I turned the door's knob and pushed it open. The waiting area inside matched the mural on the wall with more painted roses, faux cobblestones, and an oiled leather chest that stood in for a coffee table.

Paxton stood sideways to the door. He'd ditched the checkered sport coat in favor of a wrinkled shirt that bunched over the waistband of his slacks.

Lance hovered only inches away. "Why would I need a warrant? Is there something you're trying to hide?" He held a black folder and his face was rigid. Neither man seemed to notice me as I stood in the doorway.

I longed to climb the painted trellis on the wall, where I could hover near the ceiling and eavesdrop on the conversation. I'd already done that once today, so I cleared my throat instead. "Excuse me." My voice was soft compared to theirs. "Excuse me," I repeated. The men turned in unison.

"I'm sorry to interrupt." I stepped into the waiting area. "But they can probably hear you across the street."

Paxton found his voice first. "What're you doing here? I thought I told you to stay away from me and my family."

"Don't talk to her like that!" Lance pointed the folder at him. "You need to calm down, or I'm gonna haul you into the station."

"Okay, guys. That's enough." I signaled for a truce. "You two need to take it down a notch."

Lance finally lowered his arm. "She's right. And just so you know, Mr. Haney, we've cleared Missy of any involvement in your cousin's murder. Her alibi is solid for yesterday morning."

His gaze wandered to me. "Is that so? What's your alibi?"

"I was at Hank Dupre's New Year's Day breakfast. You can ask anyone who was there."

"Really?" He didn't sound convinced. "I was at Sweetwater yesterday too. That was some buffet, wasn't it? What was your favorite thing?"

"The collard greens." I knew he was testing me, but it was better to play along at this point. "Definitely not the peas. It was too early for that. I got there before nine and stayed until after ten."

"And the medical examiner put the time of death at about nine-thirty," Lance said.

Paxton's face softened almost imperceptibly. "I see. Guess I didn't pay much attention to the folks who were there yesterday."

"No problem," I said.

Lance lifted the folder once more. "It's all here in this report."

"The what?" Paxton's gaze traveled from me to the folder. "You didn't tell me anything about a report."

"You didn't give me a chance."

The man grunted and then pointed to another door, which was faux-painted to match the rest of the walls. "Let's do this in my office. Somewhere we can be alone."

He walked to the door, which was painted with swirly knots of wood, wrought-iron hinges, and a brass door knocker shaped like a lion's head. When he pushed against the animal's mane, the door swung open to reveal another suite of private offices.

The one in the corner looked like it belonged to Charlotte, since mauve paint covered the walls and an antique writing desk sat front and center. A collection of silver photo frames in all shapes and sizes filled the desk until there was no room left for actual writing. Nearby was a cherry bookcase three shelves high, lined with even more frames, and a large glass bowl filled with potpourri.

"Not that one," Paxton said. "This one." He nodded to another office. Unlike Charlotte, who favored expensive antiques and silver picture frames, his office held a mishmash of cheap oak furniture. Two file cabinets, both overflowing with folders, bookended a battered partners desk that held a glass ashtray and calculator.

I entered the room ahead of Lance and slid onto a hard-backed chair by the ashtray. Instead of bayberry oil, the smell of stale cigar smoke reached me.

"What's this about, then?" Paxton dropped heavily into a leather armchair that squeaked under his weight.

"I wanted to give you an overview of the autopsy." Lance tossed the folder on the desk before taking the chair next to me. "Remember how I told you it was blunt-force trauma? Apparently on the left side of her head, just above the ear, with some lacerations on her arm and wrist, where she fell."

I was about to interject, when I remembered my earlier promise. I'd pledged to listen and watch during the meeting, and maybe employ my "freaky sixth sense," as Lance so delicately put it.

"I'm sure it's all in there." Paxton eyed the report warily. "Probably more than we ever want to know about how she died. I get that. But that's not the most important thing." His eyes flickered over the cover. "What I really want to know—what we all want to know—is why? Why would someone do that?"

"I wish I could tell you," Lance said. "But we don't have any leads at this point, so I don't know what to say. Whoever murdered Charlotte disabled the security camera first. That tells me either they noticed the hardware, or they knew that building."

"You want to know what I think?" Paxton seemed dazed. "I think you need to talk to Susannah Wan. You know who that is, don't you?"

When Lance didn't respond, I broke my vow of silence. "She's president of the Southern Association of Wedding Planners." I turned to face Lance. "That's a group of people who plan all the weddings at the plantations and riverboats around here. Charlotte was a member before she died."

"A member?" Paxton sounded wounded. "She wasn't just a *member*. She was running for president. I think she would've won it too." Lance returned my gaze. "Did you know anything about that?"

"No, I had no idea." My mind flew back to the morning's meeting, when I first spied Suzi Wan. Normally so elegant and poised, she'd slumped by the door at Morningside as if it took every ounce of energy for her to stand upright. She didn't even greet the people who filed past her, when normally she offered a hug, an air kiss or a handshake, at the very least.

"The election is next month," Paxton said. "Everyone told Suzi she should retire and step aside so Charlotte could assume the office. But she wouldn't hear of it."

"That doesn't mean this Wan person killed her," Lance said. "We're talking about a volunteer position for a group of wedding planners, right?"

Finally, Paxton snapped out of his reverie. "You'd be surprised. It's all Suzi Wan cares about. Ever since her husband died last year, she attends every single committee meeting. Even the cleanup committee. I'm telling you, losing the election would've crushed her."

"Then why did Charlotte run?" I asked. "Your cousin doesn't seem the type who'd want to upset a widow like that."

"It was my fault," he said. "I told her to do it. Of course, I felt bad for Suzi, but it was time for her to retire. Especially since she wouldn't spend any money on the group's social media. None. Have you seen the website? It's godawful. I told Charlotte she could change all that."

Lance slowly rose and picked up the unread report. "Thank you, Mr. Haney. We'll follow up on that lead. Since you don't want to see the file, I'm taking it back with me to the station. I want you to call me, though, if you think of anything else. Anything at all."

I followed Lance's lead and rose as well. "Thanks for talking with us. And I'm really sorry about your cousin. Please let me know if there's something—anything—I can do."

He slumped in his chair now, as if talking about Charlotte had pummeled the fight right out of him. "There's nothing anyone can do. We only want the murderer to get caught. That's all."

"It's what we want too," Lance said. "Good night."

I cast a last glance at Paxton as I left the office. He didn't seem nearly as intimidating now; not like he had that morning. He looked downright miserable as he slumped in his chair. Whatever would happen to him and the business now that Charlotte was gone? He might have been its brain, but she was its soul, and something told me *she* was the reason files overflowed from the file cabinet in Paxton's office.

Chapter 10

By the time Lance and I parted ways in the atrium, the sun had sunk below the horizon, which darkened the sky to a deep plum. I left him standing by the entrance to the men's restroom, while I continued on to the exit.

I felt fine until I stumbled through the door and stomped my foot on the hard pavement. *Hell's bells!* Pain shot through my lower back. My spine was knotted like a rope, with someone tugging on the other end. Maybe a glass of Merlot, a hot bath, and an Excedrin PM would unknot it.

Do I even have painkillers? I struggled to remember as I limped past one empty parking space after another. *If worse comes to worst, I can always drive by the pharmacy on my way home and—*

"Missy! You-hoo!"

The voice stopped me cold. *Please, not again.* I turned and immediately winced.

The hazy outline of a faux-fur coat and fuzzy hat loomed before me. It was Prudence Fortenberry, and she was wearing the same getup as the day before.

"Prudence . . . what are you doing here?" I laid my hand against my heart. "Please don't scare me like that."

She giggled nervously. "Little ol' me? Why-ever would you be scared of me?"

"Because you snuck up behind me in a dark parking lot."

"I'm just headed for my car, same as you."

My hand fell away. "Really? I didn't see your car when I walked through here before. Where'd you park?"

"Behind the building." She nodded in the direction of my studio. "There was no one there, so I thought, 'why not'?"

As far as I knew, only employees parked back there. And not very many, either, what with the pitted blacktop and all. "How'd you know to park back there? Most people use the main lot when they come to the Factory."

"I've lived in Bleu Bayou my whole life, don't you know. I can tell you every parking space between here and the Mississippi River."

I tentatively took another step, anticipating the jolt of pain. "Look, I have to keep moving. My back's killing me and I really need to get home."

"Bless your heart. Let's go, then." She fell in step beside me, her sleeve brushing mine as we walked. She'd wrapped a bandage around her right hand that stretched from her fingers to her wrist.

After a moment, my car appeared up ahead. It sat all alone, with nothing on either side. "Looks like we're the last ones to leave," I said. "You never did tell me why you're here so late."

"I had to visit someone in the other building." She leaned close, as if she was about to whisper an important secret. "Actually, I came to see Bettina Leblanc. She told one of my clients they'll have to wait two weeks for an appointment. Two weeks! It's January, for heaven's sake." She finally stopped to catch her breath.

"Did it work?" I asked.

"Did *what* work?"

"Did Bettina give her an earlier appointment?"

"No, unfortunately. I couldn't do anything for her. That Bettina is quite a stickler when it comes to her wait list. You'd think she'd make an exception just this once, but she wouldn't hear of it. Oh, well. I can tell the girl I tried, anyway."

"Bless your heart, Prudence."

By now we'd arrived at my car, and a streetlamp cast a halo of light around it. I couldn't very well leave Prudence all alone in an empty parking lot, now could I?

While I longed to speed right home and uncork that bottle of Merlot, my conscience wouldn't hear of it. "Would you like a ride to your car?"

"Thank you, kindly. That'd be real nice."

She moved toward the passenger door as soon as I unlocked it with my key fob, and then she practically dove onto the passenger seat. I waited for her to awkwardly gather her coat around her before I shut my door. Although I tried to ease onto my seat, my back spasmed anyway, and I clenched my teeth.

"You poor thing." She struggled to fasten the seat belt as she spoke. "You really ought to go to a back doctor if it's bothering you that much." Finally, her seat belt clicked into place. "By the way, what are you doing here so late? I thought your studio was in the other building."

"It is. But I had an appointment with someone else too. My friend's a detective and he's working on Charlotte Devereaux's murder case. He asked me to meet with him."

A moody silence fell over us as I started up the car.

"You know, that was a terrible tragedy," she finally said. "Just terrible. Not to mention, I can't think of a worse way to go."

The silence returned as I backed out of the parking space and headed for the far corner of the building. Normally, the Factory cheered me up, with its charming brick walls, tin roof, and old-fashioned gas lamps. I especially loved it in spring, when lush pots of impatiens swung from every lamppost. Tonight, though, the building looked different. Tonight it seemed to loom in my windshield, all shrouded windows, blackened doorways, and empty flowerpots swaying in the breeze.

I drove around the building, and soon I spotted Prudence's ancient green Volvo. By the time I'd parked my car next to hers, she'd already placed her bandaged hand on the seat belt strap. The wrap slipped a bit as she struggled to undo the latch.

"Prudence?" A jagged cut tore across the tip of her right finger and continued under the bandage. The wound was gruesome, even in the dark. "What happened to you?"

She quickly pulled her hand back. When the seat belt snapped open, she flung open the passenger door and practically tumbled out of the car. "Gotta go. Thanks for the ride."

Still frantic, she fumbled to open the door to her car, and then she fell into the driver's seat. She didn't look at me as she began to pull away from the parking space.

What was that all about?

Prudence Fortenberry was a pianist, for goodness sakes. She made a living off those hands; she couldn't afford to injure one.

And the cut that ran down her finger no doubt made it impossible to play the keyboard.

Whatever the reason, she obviously didn't want to talk about it. Judging by the way she fled, she didn't want anyone else to know about it, either.

Chapter 11

Ithought about Prudence and her injured hand all the way home. She couldn't wait to escape my car and dive for the safety of hers. She wouldn't even look at me afterward. Maybe I should talk to Ambrose about it once I got back to the rent house.

Ambrose. I hadn't thought about him since I'd passed his studio on the way to the atrium. Heaven only knew how long he'd been stuck at work with his client, who just happened to look like a Victoria's Secret model.

I wearily parked my car when I got home, and then I trudged to the front door on legs of lead. Several lights glowed inside, and the *Bleu Bayou Impartial Reporter* had disappeared from our doormat. Once I opened the door and tossed my keys on a side table, I shuffled to the kitchen, where something hard *plinked* against ceramic.

It was Ambrose, who sat at our kitchen table with a bowl of something or other in front of him.

"Hey." I stepped around the farm table and plopped on the bench across from him. I'd inherited the table from my mother's side of the family, once she died, and nicks and cuts marred the surface. A new crack recently splintered the wood, but I still couldn't bear the thought of replacing it.

"Hi, there. What took you so long?" He laid his spoon down and grinned. Even at the end of a long day, his smile was genuine.

"I had a meeting with Lance and Paxton Haney." I motioned for the bowl, which he gladly nudged over. Inside were some soggy Frosted Flakes half-submerged in milk. "He's Charlotte's cousin. You know, the one who died. I also ran into Prudence Fortenberry in the parking lot. Somehow she hurt her hand." I motioned for the spoon too and scooped up some of the cereal. "It looked pretty bad. She ran away from me after I noticed it."

"You don't say. Maybe she did something stupid and she's embarrassed. She's always seemed a little strange to me anyway, to tell the truth. By the way, you got a phone call here at the house." He pulled a slip of paper from his pocket. "It was your friend, Lance. Said to call him tomorrow because he has important news for you. He said something about a 'person of interest.'"

I slowly chewed and swallowed. "Wonder who it is? And I'm surprised he didn't just call my cell."

"Really, Missy? Check your phone. My guess is your battery died hours ago and you've missed a string of calls. It wouldn't be the first time."

I started to protest but then thought better of it. "Okay, okay. How long ago did he call?"

"Only a few minutes ago. He wants to talk to you first thing in the morning." Ambrose carefully folded the note and returned it to his shirt pocket. "He keeps pulling you into these police investigations. I don't like it. I think you should let him handle it on his own. That's why they pay him."

Any other time, I would've bristled at his tone, but tonight he looked worried. "It's okay, Bo. I can handle it. He only includes me because I'm the one who keeps finding dead bodies lying around. Plus, Lance trusts me. Especially since I solved the last murder." I passed the spoon back to him as a peace offering.

"I still think you should let him handle it. I don't want you running around when there's a murderer on the loose."

"I'm not running around. And by the way—he got the autopsy report back." While Lance had made me promise not to tell anyone, this was Ambrose, after all. He was practically family. "Turns out Charlotte Devereaux had a kid before she died. Only, she never told anyone about it. That's something else that doesn't make sense."

He considered his cereal bowl. "That does seem kinda strange. Especially since you two worked together. You'd think she would've shown you a picture on her cell or something. But she never mentioned it?"

"Nope, never. Not only that, but it turns out she wanted to build up her business before she died. A lot. She planned to add a bakery, a flower shop, and a photography studio. That's what her cousin said at the meeting I went to."

"Huh. You don't say. Bet that didn't go over very well with the other business owners around here."

"Bingo. It probably made a lot people mad. They think she didn't care about them."

The mention of feelings reminded me of something else. Earlier in the day, I'd swore I'd tell Ambrose how he'd hurt my feelings in front of his client. Granted, I shouldn't have interrupted their appointment, but that didn't give him the right to pretend I wasn't there.

"There's something else I want to talk to you about." There was no time like the present. "I felt bad after I visited you at your studio today. I know you had an appointment, but you shouldn't have brushed me off like that. I'd never do that to you."

"I ignored you?"

"Yeah, you did. I even asked you to go to lunch, but you were too busy to notice."

Realization slowly dawned on his face. "You're right! I'm such a moron. But, in my defense, you know how I get when I'm working. The roof could fall in and I wouldn't notice."

"I know. That's why I didn't say anything then. But I figured if I didn't tell you about it, you'd never know how I feel."

He reached for my hand, his fingers cool from the metal spoon. "You know you can come to my studio anytime. I like it when you drop in. And I'll try to remember to show it next time."

"Thanks, Ambrose. And I'll try not to barge in when you have a client."

He squeezed my fingers before releasing them. "I've got a great idea. Why don't I take you to dinner tomorrow night to make up for it? How does that sound?"

Just when I thought I could breathe again, my lungs stalled. "Tomorrow? But tomorrow's Wednesday."

"Yeah, it is. Is there a problem?"

"As a matter of fact, there is." I could picture Beatrice, back at my studio, telling me to lie about my dinner date with Grady. Maybe not lie, exactly, but definitely not tell the truth. "I already have plans for tomorrow night. With a friend."

"A friend?"

"Yeah, um . . ." I grabbed the cereal bowl, desperate for a diversion. "Darn. We ate all of your Frosted Flakes. Want more?"

"No. No, that's okay. And what friend are we talking about?"

"An old friend. It's no big deal."

"Do I know her?"

I tried to focus, but everything seemed a little topsy-turvy. *This wasn't going at all like I'd planned.* "To tell you the truth . . . it's not a girl. I'm meeting Grady. You know, Grady from the doughnut shop."

Ambrose flinched, as if I'd sucker punched him in the stomach.

"I think he wants to talk business," I quickly added. "Run a few things by me. Probably talk about advertising and stuff . . ." I prayed I sounded more genuine than I felt.

"Grady, huh," he finally said. "Whaddya know. Well, it's no big deal. Dinner can wait 'til this weekend."

"Sure . . . this weekend. I'd love that."

Without warning, Ambrose straightened and plucked the bowl off the table. "I'd better put this away. Time for me to go to bed, anyway. I've got a big day tomorrow." He threw one leg, and then the other, over the bench and rose. "And turn out the light in here when you leave, will ya? I think you left it on last night." His voice was sharp now.

"I did? Okay, if you say so."

He strode to the sink, where he roughly tossed the bowl in the basin. By the time it finally stopped clattering, he was gone.

"Good night," I called after him.

No sound, so I dropped my head to the table. *Why, oh why, didn't I listen to Beatrice?* What made me run off at the mouth like that? He was obviously upset. I should've stayed quiet and let him guess who was meeting me for dinner tomorrow night.

Now it was too late. Like so many times before, I'd let my mouth take off before my brain had a chance to catch up.

I rose from the table with a sigh, and then I slapped at the light switch on the kitchen wall. Once I made my way down the hall and into my bedroom, I tossed on a tattered T-shirt and flowered boxer shorts. A few halfhearted passes with a washcloth and toothbrush later, I fell into bed with a *thump*.

My mind kept replaying the scene with Ambrose in the kitchen. He looked *so* sad. Disappointed, even. He'd actually blanched at the news.

Every time I tried to get comfortable, my mattress turned rock-hard. When I flipped right, it pressed against my ribs. When I turned left, my shoulder met granite.

Finally, after hours of tossing and turning, and maybe a few measly hours of sleep, I gave up and swung my legs over the side of the bed. A ribbon of pink glowed under the window shade in my room. Ready or not, dawn had arrived, so I quietly rose and padded down the hall. Nothing sounded but a few starlings in the backyard as they called to the morning sun.

Phew. Phew. Phew. Normally, I enjoyed the sound of birdcalls, but today it was a little too loud and a little too incessant for its own good. I tried to ignore it as I walked to the kitchen, where my gaze instantly flew to a hook near the telephone, where Ambrose always kept his keys. *Empty.* Not only that, but the countertop was spotless. Every other morning, for as long as I could remember, Ambrose left a watery coffee-cup stain near the stove. He also scattered sugar crystals on the stainless-steel burners when he added two teaspoons—never more and never less—to his coffee cup. Today, though, everything was sparkling.

Now I felt even worse. Apparently, he'd rather leave early, and without his coffee, than risk running into me. I trudged back to my bedroom on legs of lead.

Frowning, I flung open the closet door and quickly grabbed the first thing I saw: a black turtleneck, burgundy corduroys, and dark kitten heels. Once dressed, I moved to the bathroom to assess the damage.

The face in the mirror looked pale and puffy. Dark rings circled both eyes, which made my winter pallor even more noticeable, so I first dabbed some under-eye concealer over the shadows. Then I added blush, mascara, and lipstick, although nothing seemed to help much.

Maybe what I needed was a good hairdo. The French knot seemed to work reasonably well yesterday, at least for part of the day, so I quickly gathered my hair into a ponytail, twisted it from top to bottom, and then coiled the strands at the base of my neck.

That helped some, but not much. What I needed was a foolproof pick-me-up: a great hat. So I shuffled back to the closet and plucked one of my favorites from the top shelf.

A wine-colored fascinator made of wool, it featured Lady Amherst's pheasant feathers at the sides and a pouf of black netting on top. Best of all, the French knot would play peekaboo under the rim of the fascinator and give people behind me something to look at.

Once I angled the hat against the side of my head, I poked a hatpin through it. *Much better.* I hightailed it out of the bedroom, grabbed my keys from the side table in the entry hall, and stepped outside.

A light drizzle misted everything. Thank goodness, I'd opted for the sturdy wool fascinator, instead of a more delicate one made of silk or velvet.

To be safe, I cupped my hands over the feathers and dashed for my car. As soon as I reached it, I started up the engine and pulled away, just as a few raindrops landed on the hood.

The rain grew stronger as I pulled onto the highway. Lulled by the staccato sound of water pelting metal, my thoughts slipped back to the night before: To the way Ambrose smiled at me when I first came home. And the way he teased me about my cell phone battery. Even the way he worried about me, once he read the note from Lance aloud. He'd said something about a "person of interest" in Charlotte Devereaux's murder investigation, which was about the only good thing to come from our conversation.

It meant Lance finally had a lead in the case. While not as solid as a suspect, a "person of interest" meant he had a starting point. I'd have to call him as soon as I got to the Factory, before anything else could distract me.

As if on cue, the Factory's parking lot appeared up ahead. I spied Ambrose's Audi in the third row, so I cautiously pulled into the row before it. There was no sign of Bettina's car, but, then again, she might've carpooled to work this morning.

What with the ominous clouds overhead, I made sure to double-check the latch on the soft-top after I shut off the car.

Knock, knock, knock.

Sweet baby Jesus. My heart leaped to my throat. Stormie Lanai appeared in my window, larger than life and covered in stage makeup. She wore thick fuchsia lipstick, charcoal eyeliner, and false eyelashes that fluttered like two butterfly wings.

Whatever was Stormie doing in the parking lot of the Factory at six in the morning?

I cautiously lowered the automatic window. Luckily, the rain had slackened and only a few drops fell against the steering wheel. "Can I help you?" I didn't mean to bark, but she'd scared the bejesus out of me. "Good morning. Stormie Lanai here. Can we talk?"

My first instinct was to jam the car in reverse and roar away, but then she'd only follow me. It made more sense to face her in public—even though the parking lot was practically empty—than to meet her back at my rent house, where we'd definitely be alone.

I sighed, raised the window, and whisked out the keys. Then I threw open the door and stepped onto the pavement, as she shoved a handheld mic under my chin. Along with thick makeup, she wore a tight plaid jacket, a skirt that was two sizes too small, and a pair of stilettos that added six inches to her height. All in all, it was hard not to stare.

Behind her stood a middle-aged cameraman with a JVC recorder on his shoulder, which he switched on the moment the reporter began her countdown.

"On *one*: Three . . . two . . . one. This is Stormie Lanai—"

"Just a second." I threw up my hand to block the camera lens.

"What're you doing?" Stormie demanded.

"I've got a few questions for you first. How'd you know where to find me?"

"I wasn't sure, but I ran into your assistant yesterday. She told me you come to work pretty early."

Poor Beatrice. The sound of a whirring camera probably caught her off guard too. "Fine. But don't go back to my studio." I lowered my hand. "You won't find anything there. You'll only upset my assistant. If you have something to say, say it to me . . . not her."

"That's why I'm here, honey," Stormie said, a little too sweetly. "To get your side of the story. That's what you want folks to know about, right?"

She has a point. Especially since Lance had identified a person of interest in the case. Maybe it was time for me to launch a public defense and finally clear my name. It might help convince my clients they shouldn't cancel on me. "All right. You win. What do you want to know?"

The cameraman repositioned the camera.

"On *one*," Stormie repeated. "Three . . . two . . . one. This is Stormie Lanai, reporting live for KATZ news."

A thunderclap sounded overhead, but we all ignored it.

"I'm standing here today with Melissa DuBois, owner of a well-known millinery studio," Stormie said. "We're at a shopping center called the Factory, where police found the body of a wedding planner two days ago. So, Missy . . ." She turned a fraction, no doubt because that favored her better side. "Can you tell us what happened that morning?"

I did my best to ignore the blinking red light on the camera. "The victim was already dead by the time I arrived at work. I found her in a barrel behind my studio."

"It was *your* barrel, wasn't it?" Stormie widened her eyes dramatically, which stopped the oversized lashes from fluttering. "It was a *whiskey* barrel, from what I understand."

"Well, yes. It was my barrel. But I only put it there to catch the rain."

She inched the microphone closer. "Police say the victim was bludgeoned to death with something you'd made. Isn't that right?"

"No. I mean, yes. It was my hat stand. But they found it in a dumpster."

Her eyes widened even more. "So, whoever murdered the poor victim just tossed it away, like a scrap of trash?"

A light sweat broke out along my hairline. "Look, I've already been cleared by the police, if that's what you're getting at."

"I'm not *getting at* anything." She glanced at the camera sincerely. "But our viewers have a right to know what happened, don't they?"

Words failed me. Maybe it was the blinking light on top of the JVC or the ridiculously long lashes that hung over the reporter's eyes, but I couldn't focus.

"Well, don't you have anything to say to our viewers?" she asked.

"Look . . . um, what happened was—I mean, the whole reason I was there—um . . ."

She whisked the microphone away. "How horrible to find a dead body in the parking lot behind where you work. And then to know you made the murder weapon . . . well, it's all too tragic. This is Stormie Lanai reporting live—"

It's now or never. I grabbed the microphone back. "Look. I've given the police my alibi, which they've confirmed. From what I understand, they identified a person of interest last night. You might want to double-check your information before you ambush someone again."

Her mouth fell open. "I didn't—"

"One more thing," I said. "Don't ever harass my assistant again." Only then did I relinquish the mic.

Stormie looked dazed. As she whirled away from me, her stiletto splashed into a puddle of oil and muck, and she quickly whisked it up again.

Then she and her cameraman began to stalk across the parking lot, apparently headed for a royal blue Republic trash dumpster that partially blocked a white van. No wonder I hadn't seen the news van when I first pulled into the parking lot.

They both disappeared from view a short while later. Although the day had just begun, I already wanted to go home.

Chapter 12

By the time the reporter zoomed away from the parking lot with her cameraman, the drizzle had hardened to rain. I locked up my car, and then I scampered through the parking lot, too rushed to worry about protecting my hat this time.

Sure enough, by the time I passed the atrium, where sheet after sheet of rain slid down the windows, a limp feather drooped against my cheek.

My only hope to preserve what was left of my outfit was to dash under an overhang that jutted from the building. Which helped some, but not enough, since wind whipped the rain sideways and splashed it onto my legs and feet. By the time I finally arrived at the studio, wet corduroy hugged my thighs like a clammy paper sack.

It wasn't my only problem, though. A pile of glass shards greeted me, in a spot where I normally kept a welcome mat. The glass belonged to my beautiful French door, which had been reduced to rubble. Most of the shards were no bigger than my fingernail.

To add insult to injury, the debris breeched the doorjamb and spilled onto a rug inside. I blindly crouched to brush away some shards. *Ouch.* I pulled back, but it was too late: a jagged piece jutted from my palm like an icy thorn.

Nothing made sense. I could understand one pane of broken glass. Maybe the wind blew something against it; that was understandable. But all fifteen window panes? It was too much. Especially since some gouges on the doorframe looked suspiciously like ax marks.

The landscape tilted as I rose. Sometime during the night, as I tossed and turned only a few miles away, an intruder hacked away at my French door, methodically smashing each and every window-pane. Looking through raindrops at the carnage, nothing made sense, at least not right away.

I finally glanced up to see Ambrose standing beside me.

"What happened?" he whispered.

"I—I don't know. I just got here."

He helped me rise, and then he gently turned me away from the carnage. "Do you have any idea who did this?"

I shook my head, too numb to speak.

"Wait here a second." He pushed open what was left of the door and stepped onto the throw rug inside.

"No, Ambrose. Don't. They still could be in there."

He moved quickly, though, as he lurched over the rug.

"Please, don't." I lunged after him and caught the hem of his jacket. "Please let the police handle this."

"But I don't want them to get away."

I let go of the hem when I realized I'd left a bloody smear. "They could be armed. I'll call Lance. He'll know what to do."

That stopped him, and he hovered in place for a moment. "All right." He retreated through the doorway. "We'll go to my place and you can call your friend from there."

We somberly made our way next door. Once we reached Ambrose's Allure Couture, he held open the door for me and then closed and locked it when we were safely inside. His eyes widened when he noticed something. "Look at you. You're hurt. Stay right there."

He left me to retrieve a Band-Aid from a first-aid kit he kept under the counter. By the time he returned, a pink trail of blood curled around my wrist.

He wiped it away with a tissue and carefully applied a bandage. "That's much better."

"Thank you." While I hated to move, I needed to call Lance. Once I withdrew my cell and tapped its screen, Lance's voice sounded over the receiver.

"Hey, there. You got my message."

"Can you come to my studio?"

"I dunno. Lots of things going on here and—"

"It's an emergency, Lance." Thank goodness he and I were such good friends. Over the years, we'd learned to communicate in shorthand, and now neither one minded when the other one interrupted. "Someone broke into my studio last night. Shattered my French door. Glass everywhere."

"Are you okay?"

"Yeah, but I don't know if they're still there." My eyes flew to Ambrose. "Thank goodness Ambrose found me. I'm calling you from his studio."

"Gotcha. I'll call for backup and then head over to the Factory. Don't move, okay?"

I couldn't help but sigh, in spite of everything. "You always say that to me, Lance. Just where am I supposed to go?"

"With you, there's no telling. And I'll be there in five minutes. Promise you won't go back to your own studio."

"Scout's honor." I threw Ambrose a look as I clicked off the line and laid the phone down.

"What?"

"Lance told me to stay away from my studio. I knew it was a bad idea for you to go back inside."

"Hey, I was worried about you. What can I say? At least you're safe now."

He pulled out a stool for me, which I gladly accepted. Amazing how quickly things changed. We'd both gone to bed angry the night before, but now it didn't matter.

"Look, I'm sorry about last night," I said. "I hated how we left things."

"Me too. I didn't sleep at all."

"I didn't want to hurt your feelings, Ambrose. But we never said we'd only date each other." I purposefully studied the Band-Aid so I wouldn't have to look into his beautiful, Tiffany-blue eyes.

"No, it's my fault. I should've told you if it bothered me."

If. The word hung awkwardly in the air. *What does he mean by that?* I was about to ask when he turned away.

He spoke over his shoulder as he walked. "You're soaking wet. Might as well get you cleaned up." He moved to the back of the room, where he paused in front of an antique armoire called a *chifforobe*. "There's bound to be a slip or a skirt in here you can wear."

I slid from the stool and followed him. Like most designers, Ambrose kept a "hide closet" in the back of his studio to stash away the messier parts of his profession.

His version of a hide closet was a maple chifforobe with a rounded top. When he pulled open its doors, a bolt of fabric, tub of scissors, and poufy ball-gown skirt tumbled to the ground. He plucked up the skirt and tossed it to me. "Here, try this."

I slid the skirt over my wet cords. Then I unzipped the pants and kicked them aside. The skirt didn't quite fit over my hips, so I used a safety pin I found on the waistband to cinch the fabric together. "Jiminy cricket, Ambrose. What size is this thing?"

"Double zero. It's from a fashion show I did a few months back."

I tried my best to pin the skirt before moving to a mirror that hung by the armoire. The fabric ballooned around me like an upside-down teacup, which made us both smile. I played up the moment and spun around and around, until the floor tilted crazily and I wobbled to a stop.

Inspired now, I lunged through a few modeling poses—complete with exaggerated backbends and pouty lips—which brought on some belly laughs. By the time someone knocked at the door, he and I were both beside ourselves.

He quickly sobered, though. "Lance must be here."

I gathered up the excess fabric and hurried behind him as he headed for the door. The minute he swung it open, Lance rushed in.

"Are you okay?" he asked.

"Yeah, I'm fine. Thanks for coming so quickly. You must have a thousand things—"

"Don't mention it." He suddenly paused. "Playing dress up?"

"What?" I glanced down. "This thing? My pants got soaked in the rain. Ambrose loaned it to me."

"Lovely." He nodded to Bo. "Do you guys have any idea what happened next door? By the way, whoever did it wasn't very subtle."

"That's what I thought." I dropped the folds of taffeta, which quickly swallowed my feet. "It's completely destroyed. But I have no idea who's responsible."

"It must have something to do with the murder investigation. It has to. One of my guys just radioed from your shop and said it doesn't look like they took anything. Cash register's still there, and so is a key you stashed under it. By the way, you might want to find a better hiding place for that."

I met him at the counter while he spoke. "About the only person I can think of who's angry with me is Stormie Lanai. You know, the KATZ reporter. She ambushed me in the parking lot this morning."

"She did?" Ambrose's eyes widened. "Why didn't you tell me?"

"We were kinda busy, what with the door and all. But, yeah. She shoved a microphone at me and asked a lot of questions."

"She can't do that," Lance said. "She's on private property. Unless your landlord gave her permission."

"Knowing my landlord, he didn't." I pulled out one of the bar stools and settled onto it, which pooled the fabric up and over its sides. "But I don't think she'll be using footage from the interview anyway. I kinda turned the tables on her."

"Missy!" Ambrose did his best to look stern, but a smile broached his lips. "You know it's not a good idea to piss off a news reporter."

"I didn't *try*, obviously. It just kinda happened."

"Let's get back to the door." Lance took the stool next to mine. "The point is someone wants to send you a message. There's no doubt about that." He reached into his pocket and pulled out a notepad, along with a ballpoint pen. "Now, start at the beginning and tell me everything that happened. I'll have to write up an incident report when I get back to the station."

I provided a quick rundown of everything that happened before my grisly discovery that morning. Once I finished, Lance flipped the notepad closed.

"I still think it has something to do with the murder investigation," he said. "By now, everyone knows the victim died behind your studio and the killer used something of yours."

"You're probably right. By the way, Ambrose told me you called last night. He said you have a person of interest. Who is it?"

"Ah, that." He quickly slid the pen and notepad into his pocket. "There's a baker in your complex by the name of Bettina Leblanc. Do you know her?"

"Yeah, I do." I shivered, but it had nothing to do with the damp turtleneck or my soaked kitten heels. "She owns a bakery upstairs called Pink Cake Boxes. I saw her yesterday."

"Well, we got a tip about her last night. Turns out someone saw her arguing with Charlotte Devereaux the night before the murder. They were both at a local restaurant. You'll never guess who called in the tip."

I couldn't help but shiver again. He must be talking about his mother, Odilia LaPorte. Mrs. LaPorte owned one of the most popular restaurants in town. "Don't tell me . . . your mom heard them having a fight."

He nodded. "Yep. On Sunday, New Year's Eve. Apparently, they got into it in a hallway at her place."

"But I can't believe Bettina would do something like that." I spoke slowly, trying to absorb the news. "I *don't* believe it. Did you take her into custody?"

"No, she's not a suspect yet. And we don't have an arrest warrant. At this point she's cooperating; she came into the station last night on her own."

I didn't mean to hog the conversation with Lance, but now he had me worried. "How'd she explain herself?"

"She couldn't, not really. Just said something about them both having too much to drink the night before the murder. Said they got carried away at the restaurant."

I lowered my voice. "But you know that's not true, Lance. According to the coroner's report, Charlotte only had one or two drinks the night before she died."

"Bingo. That's why we're checking out Leblanc's history. Maybe she had some prior conflicts with the victim."

"Was there video?" Finally, Ambrose got a word in edgewise. "Maybe a surveillance tape that caught something?"

"Unfortunately, no." Lance leaned back on the stool. "My mom couldn't afford a bunch of cameras when she first opened. She only has three: in the kitchen, the dining room, and the parking lot. Since I don't have visual proof, I'm going to focus on Leblanc's statement. Maybe the two women didn't get along."

"I doubt it," I said. "They were pretty chummy. They even belonged to the same trade group. It's called the Southern Association of Wedding Planners—I think I told you about 'em."

"You did. Which means I've gotta go back to the station and do some research when we're done here."

"But what's next for Bettina?" I couldn't bear the thought of her twisting in the wind like this.

"Like I told you, she was free to go last night." Lance quickly rose. "I imagine she's called an attorney by now. That's what I would've done."

"Good point. Is there anything I can do? Anything at all."

"No. Not yet. And it seems like you have your hands full here. My guys are pulling prints from your studio, and they'll run them through the system. In the meantime, I'll fill out the incident report."

"And I'll get some plywood," Ambrose said. "It might not be pretty, but it'll keep the rain out until we can get you a new door."

Which is all well and good, but not the perfect answer. "I appreciate that, Ambrose. I really do. But how will my customers get in then?"

"I hadn't thought of that." He stared at the wall that ran between our studios for a moment, as if he could see right through it. "Guess they can't. Maybe you should work here for a while. There's enough room for both of us."

"That's very nice of you, Bo." While I appreciated the sweet gesture, it posed yet another problem. "But what about Beatrice?" I couldn't afford to give my assistant a day off, and she couldn't afford to take one, since she needed the money as much as the rest of us.

"Why doesn't she work from home?" Lance offered.

"Great idea." I nodded my thanks to him. "I'll tell her to work at her apartment today."

"And I'll make some room for you here," Ambrose said. "I've got a drafting table in the back and some extra supplies. You'll probably need some stuff from your place, though, so I won't nail the plywood down just yet. I'm sure you'd rather not use your back door, since it opens onto a crime scene."

"Thanks, Ambrose." A lump began to form at the back of my throat. "That means a lot to me. And after everything that happened last night—"

"It's okay." He quickly glanced from me to Lance. "We don't have to talk about it right now. Let's get everything cleaned up outside your studio and make sure you're safe. The rest of it can wait."

"All right, then." Lance stepped away from the counter. "Sounds like you two have a plan. But call me if you see anything suspicious. In the meantime, we'll run the prints and I'll check out Bettina Leblanc's history."

Chapter 13

Lance hurried to the exit and soon he disappeared. Only then did I check the time on my cell phone, which lay on the counter. It was already seven, which meant I'd been at the Factory for nearly half an hour. Not only that, but I hadn't had a single cup of coffee and my brain felt like mush.

"Say, Bo." I turned to him. "I haven't had any coffee yet. Think I'll get some from the Starbucks counter in the lobby." *What's another five minutes in the grand scheme of things?* "Do you want any?"

"No, I'm okay."

"I'll be back in a few minutes."

I quickly rose and made my way to the door. Even though Lance probably wouldn't approve, I didn't see how a few measly minutes in the lobby could change anything. After all, he'd mentioned my studio was empty, so whoever ruined the entrance was long gone.

Once I stepped outside, a weak splash of sunshine fell on my shoulders. I purposefully turned away from the pile of rubble outside my door—no need to revisit the carnage—and tried to ignore the images that ping-ponged through my mind: smashed glass, gouged wood, and a useless nail protruding from a broken door hinge.

I wanted to focus on other things instead: Like the ray of sun on my shoulders. The slippery feel of a damp quill on my cheek. The new cars that now worked their way into the parking lot at the Factory.

Although it was only seven, several more cars had parked near the businesses that kept early-morning hours. The flower shop, for one, opened at the crack of dawn, since Dana LeBoeuf accepted deliveries then. No doubt she was stationed in the alley at this very moment, telling a driver where to stash a box of hydrangeas in her walk-in cooler.

Another early bird was Brooke Champagne. The photographer often arrived at daybreak to shoot her subjects in the soft morning light. The rain must have changed her schedule, though, since nothing stirred inside Brooke's Bridal Portraits when I passed by.

A few moments later, I arrived at the atrium and swung open the plate-glass door. The heavenly scent of newly roasted coffee beans reached me the moment I stepped inside.

"Hello, there."

I whirled around to see Suzi Wan. Today she wore another chic Chanel suit, only this time the color was teal, not red. She'd accessorized it with black Tahitian pearls and matching earrings. While she seemed to have recovered from the day before, dark rings still circled her eyes.

"Hello, Miss Wan."

"Wherever are you going dressed like that, my dear?"

"Huh?" Then I remembered the taffeta ball-gown skirt. "You mean the skirt? I had to borrow it from my friend, Ambrose. He doesn't wear it, of course. But once I took off my pants . . ." My voice trailed off, since I was only digging the hole deeper.

"Don't worry about it, dear." Finally, Suzi's gaze came 'round to my face. "No need to explain. I love taffeta."

"My choice was either this or a slip."

"Then it looks like you made the right choice," she said. "Bless your heart."

Maybe now would be a good time to change the subject. "I saw you at the meeting yesterday." While still awkward, I couldn't think of anything else to say. "I sat near the front. Maybe you saw me too."

"I did. Thank you for coming and supporting our group like that."

"My pleasure. Usually I look forward to those meetings. But yesterday was different. I can only imagine how hard it was for you to give that speech."

"You mean when I talked about Charlotte? You have no idea." Suzi fell silent, which only magnified the *whhhiiirrr* of an espresso machine across the way.

"Everyone loved her. I'm sure her death surprised a lot of people."

"No doubt. And I hated to be the one to have to tell them. I didn't have much choice, though, did I? It's all part of being the group's president. To be honest, sometimes I wonder why I bother."

The minute she mentioned being president, my mind returned to a different conversation. To last night's meeting with Paxton Haney, where he talked about the upcoming election.

"Say . . . I heard something interesting yesterday. Paxton Haney told me your members have to vote next month. He said you're running for president again."

"He did, did he?"

I didn't mean to pry, but she'd been the one to bring up the Southern Association of Wedding Planners. "Yes, he did."

"Well, he's right. And someone had the nerve to run against me. Believe it or not, it was Charlotte, God rest her soul. She thought we needed new blood on the board of directors. Which couldn't be further from the truth."

"Hmmm. Were you worried about it?"

"Not really." Now Suzi pursed her lips, as if the words were bitter. "I thought she was in for a rude awakening. I've held that office for over a decade, you know. For her to come in and challenge me like that . . . well, it *wasn't* very gracious."

Obviously I'd opened a can of worms, and it'd take a soothing response to close it up again. "Ten years *is* a long time. I'm sure you've done an excellent job."

"Thank you, dear. I try. But some things can't be learned overnight. Charlotte didn't know anything about the politics involved."

Now I truly regretted bringing up the subject. Not only that, but the *pppffftt* of another machine called out to me from the coffee bar. "I should probably order my drink, since I need to get back to my friend's studio."

"You do that. I'm done with my visit here, anyway. Unfortunately, I had to leave one of my clients a little early, since I'm backed up after yesterday." She hastily glanced at the exit. "Guess I'll see you at the next meeting."

I cocked my head. "Actually, I think we'll meet up before then. I've decided to go to Charlotte's funeral. Remember? It's on Friday."

"Yes, there's that." Suzi waved nonchalantly. "Don't think I can make it. I've got too much to do. It's a shame, really, but sometimes these things can't be helped. See you later." She suddenly pivoted and took a step toward the door. When she reached it, she fumbled with the wrong end of the push bar before she realized her mistake, and then she flung it open.

If that didn't beat all. I watched her leave until the ache between my temples brought me back to the present. Thankfully, a barista stood at the coffee counter, and she looked ready to take my order.

I ambled over to her and politely requested a tall, no-whip white mocha. Then she and I chatted about this, that, and the other thing, while she busied herself with the machines. At one point, the *pppfffttt* of the steamer drowned out our voices altogether. That was when I glanced over my shoulder and noticed someone new was walking through the entrance to the atrium.

It was Hank Dupre, of all people. Beatrice's uncle and my host at the New Year's Day breakfast sauntered through the door wearing a different, although equally loud, dress shirt.

"Hello, Mr. Dupre," I called out. No need to worry about the taffeta ball-gown skirt with him, since his crimson shirt looked like something a matador might like.

"Hello." He approached me. "If I've told you once, I've told you a thousand times: It's Hank. Mr. Dupre is my dad."

"Of course. I'm sorry. I just forgot." By this time, my drink was ready and the barista passed it to me over the counter.

"Good to see you at my party the other day. Hope you liked the food."

"How could I not? Ruby's a great cook." I snuck a sip of coffee, which was hot and strong. "This hits the spot."

"You're not a morning person, are you?" He chuckled. "I just came in for a meeting, but I thought I'd be the only one here."

"You'd be surprised. Some of the shop owners get up pretty early. And I'm so glad I did this morning. My front door got smashed last night. Clean blown to pieces."

His eyebrows shot up. "That's terrible. Who did it?"

"I don't know. They were brutal too. I'm using Ambrose's shop next door until I can get mine fixed."

"I know someone who can fix it for you." He broke away from our conversation to order a coffee of the day from the barista, before he started up again. "Anyway, it's the guy who rehabs my residential properties. He's a whiz with a skill saw."

"That'd be great! Otherwise I have to find someone off the Internet."

"Nah, don't fool with that. I'll send you his name as soon as I get back to my office."

While he spoke, I snuck another sip from my coffee cup, which was so good I almost hated to swallow it. "Thanks. I'd like to get it fixed today, what with the rainstorms and all. Speaking of which . . . what brought you out on such a crummy day?"

"I'm helping one of the guys upstairs sell a business. He wants to retire soon."

"Good for him. But I didn't know you did that kind of thing. I thought you only sold residential real estate."

"That's my main business." He passed some money across the counter. "But I also work with company owners on the side. Got my law degree way-back-when from LSU before I took the real estate exam. Some of the old-timers around here remember that."

"So you can draw up contracts. That's good to know."

"They're a little more tricky than loan docs, but yeah. My client is selling a special events company, so we're talking mostly about intangible assets. Things like contracts and contact sheets."

"A special events company?" *It can't be, can it?* "You don't mean Paxton Haney, do you? He owns Happily Ever After Events upstairs."

Hank nodded. "That's him. He's in a hurry too. Said he would've sold out a long time ago, but his cousin wouldn't hear of it."

Well, saddle me up and call me a horse. "I had no idea." I purposefully took another sip from the cup to buy a little time. If Paxton Haney wanted to sell the business and Charlotte wanted to expand it, I could only imagine the fireworks that flew between those two. "But isn't there a waiting period when a partner dies? Charlotte just passed away."

"Normally there is," he said, "but she rewrote her will to name Mr. Haney the business's designee. He'll have to wait until after the reading, of course, but it looks like he can sell it without anyone's blessing."

"You don't say." I carefully shifted the cup to my other hand. No telling what Lance would think about *that* bit of information. He needed to know—and the sooner, the better. "Well, I've gotta get going. Will I see you Friday at the memorial service?"

"You bet. Wouldn't miss it."

I waved good-bye and began to walk away. Of all the strange things to hear this morning, I never expected to find out Paxton Haney wanted to sell Happily Ever After Events. Why would he do that so soon after Charlotte's death? It didn't sound like something a cousin would do.

Tucking my skirt in close, I walked across the lobby with my gaze lowered until I reached the exit and glanced up. Sheet after sheet of rainwater rolled down the atrium's windows like a clear shade set free of its roller. Wave upon wave, with no end in sight.

Dagnabit. I'd have to slosh through a downpour again. Unlike other parts of the Factory, Ambrose's studio wasn't reachable by an interior hall. It only had two doors: the main one off the parking lot and an employees' entrance that led to the back lot.

Looks like I'd get drenched again. Not to mention, I'd surely ruin Ambrose's taffeta skirt this time. How could I return a ball-gown skirt to him with pockmarks across the front? It wouldn't be very polite, and it'd ruin any chance I had of borrowing something else in the future. Maybe I should just stay put and call Lance from the lobby, where at least I'd be warm and dry.

I reached for my cell, which I seemed to remember stashing in the skirt's hidden pocket, but felt only fabric. *Sweet mother of pearl.* I must've left the phone on Ambrose's counter. Now I had no way to reach Lance . . . or did I?

I spun around, hoping to find Hank by the coffee bar. *No such luck.* He must've taken his coffee—and his cell phone—with him to the car. He was probably in a hurry to get back to his office and the paperwork for Paxton Haney's business.

My gaze took in nothing but yards and yards of empty space, which ended at the open elevator across the way. It was the same car I'd ridden the night before, when I rushed upstairs to meet Lance at Happily Ever After Events. The business lay directly across from Pink Cake Boxes, the bakery started by Bettina Leblanc.

Bettina. I hadn't thought of her since yesterday, when Lance mentioned she was the person of interest in Charlotte's murder case. I could only imagine how horrible she felt when he gave her the news.

Maybe I should pay her a visit. Even though she might not be at the bakery today, since she spent part of the night before at the police station, I wouldn't put it past her, knowing how hard she worked. She'd also have a phone I could borrow. I changed tack and trudged across the floor to where the empty elevator stood waiting for me. By now, nothing would surprise me.

Chapter 14

Once the elevator swept me to the second floor, it deposited me in the hall lined with framed produce labels. No time to dillydally this morning, though, since my sights were set on Bettina's bakery, which lay all the way at the end.

A rectangle of light fell on the carpet in front of it. When I reached the bakery, I spied someone inside, but it wasn't Bettina. The girl sat at one of the tables, with her back to the door and her hand on a photo album. A mink coat lay over the chair next to hers, topped by a pair of matching gloves. The fur's sheen matched the glimmer in the girl's coal-black hair.

Only one person I knew could afford a full-length Russian sable with rounded collar and cuffs, not to mention the matching gloves.

"Trudi?"

She spun around. "Huh, hello." After a second, her gaze drifted south, just like Suzi Wan's had done. "Aren't you a little dressed up for this weather?"

"It's a long story. I'm just borrowing the skirt for the day." Although I didn't see Bettina, she might return at any moment. "Mind if I join you?"

"I guess not . . . if you *must*." She sighed and pushed the coat off the chair, where it landed on the floor and rounded like a sleeping bear.

"Thanks." I sat next to her. Apparently, she'd been studying pictures of wedding cakes in the photo albums. Tall cakes, wide cakes, some five stories high. A sticky note jutted from one of the pages like a yellow caution sign. "Looking at wedding cakes?"

"Obviously."

Once again, her tone seemed to question my intelligence, but I ignored it. "That one's beautiful." A photo showed an elaborate wedding cake bound with garlands of rhinestones, crystals, and delicate seed pearls. "But I thought you canceled your wedding."

"I did. But my boyfriend convinced me to change my mind."

"You don't say. So, now you have to plan everything all over again?"

"Unfortunately, yes. But this time I'm going to do it right. By the way, you *do* know you're the one who introduced us to Charlotte Devereaux, don't you?"

"I did?" *Something else I'd forgotten.* Usually, a bride found me through her wedding planner, but this time everything got turned around. Trudi came to me first, and then I introduced her and her fiancé to Charlotte. "I hope you don't blame me for introducing y'all. I had no idea this would happen."

"It's all water under the bridge now." She lightly grazed the photo with her fingernail. "Luckily, this town is crawling with wedding planners. Since I'm having it at Morningside Plantation, they were only too happy to suggest someone new."

My mind clicked into overdrive. While I didn't want to be pushy, or downplay what happened to Charlotte, I might not get the chance to talk wedding veils with Trudi Whidbee again. "I still have the design for your veil, you know. I could easily dust it off." Not only that, but yesterday's bride wasn't the least bit interested in her cathedral-length veil, and I hated to let a perfectly good design go to waste.

"Here's the deal." Trudi ran her nail over the photo again, but this time it left a mark. "I've picked out an entirely different gown. I'm starting fresh. It's a mermaid dress, which wouldn't work with your design."

"Maybe." I tried to sound casual, but my mind whirled with possibilities. A mermaid gown cried out for an angel-cut veil, which draped down the sides. "I can always come up with something new. What if we—"

"That won't be necessary." Trudi tried to rub the scratch away with her thumb, but it didn't budge. "I've given my new wedding planner free reign to pick out the vendors this time. And I already wrote you a check for your design. The way I see it, we're even steven."

She quickly rose and snatched the sleeping coat off the ground.

"Tell Miss Leblanc I couldn't wait for her anymore. She was supposed to be gone a minute, but that was five minutes ago. I don't have time for this."

Although I'd obviously annoyed her, I couldn't help myself. "One last question."

"What now?"

"You said you hired a new wedding planner. Who'd you pick?"

"Not that it's any of your business—" she shrugged into the coat, which swallowed her whole—"but I'm using Suzi Wan." As her right arm entered the sleeve, something flashed; a spark of light from the diamond Rolex on her wrist, which she quickly checked. "Great. Now it's been six minutes. *This* is why I need a good wedding planner."

"I'll tell Bettina you had to leave. I'm sure she'll understand." There was no need to be ugly with her, even though she'd given me nothing but snippy replies.

"Whatever. Tell her to call Miss Wan next time. I marked my favorite in the photo album, and they can work out the details."

She swept away, the bulky coat receding after her. The last bit to leave was the hem of a side pelt.

Funny, but Suzi didn't say anything about working with Trudi Whidbee when we spoke in the lobby. Apparently, she didn't find it newsworthy, even though Trudi came from one of the richest families in Louisiana. That girl was the ultimate "get" for a wedding planner, and surely Suzi knew that.

Come to think of it . . . no wonder Suzi was at the Factory so early. She told me she'd come for a client meeting, but she never said which client.

I pondered that while I waited for Bettina to reappear. After a moment, the baker skulked through a side door and entered the room.

She looked exhausted. Her gray braid straggled onto the shoulders of the chef's coat, which hadn't seen an iron in several days. She'd also forgotten one of the buttons, and her pale skin showed through the gap. If I didn't know better, I'd have sworn Bettina spent the night curled up next to her mixing bowls.

"Missy?" She held a sketch pad, which she lowered when she saw me. "Where's Trudi?"

"She had to leave." I plastered on a bright smile; no need to start her day off on the wrong foot. "She apologized to high heavens, though.

Said something about her wedding planner calling you later. Speaking of which . . . do you have a phone I can borrow?"

"I'm afraid I left it in my car. My landline went out last night, so I was going to go get it once the rain let up." Bettina shrugged and tossed the sketch pad on the nearest surface. The waist–high display case held cake samples and a half-dozen wedding cake toppers, complete with frosted rosettes and white-chocolate hearts. I asked Bettina about the samples once, since I couldn't imagine they stayed fresh for more than a week or so. That was when she confessed the "cakes" were actually Styrofoam discs frosted with spackle.

I patted the chair next to me, which still was warm from Trudi's backside. "You look exhausted."

She wearily took me up on my offer and slumped into the chair. "That girl told me she wanted to see a cake I'm making for the governor's niece. Guess she wasn't really interested, after all." Her red-rimmed eyes grew narrow. "To tell you the truth, it's probably for the best. I'm not sure I could deal with her kind today."

Although it was obvious, I had to ask. "How're you doing this morning, Bettina?"

"I'm pretty tired, that's for sure."

"Lance told me what happened last night."

"So you know. I can't believe this is happening to me."

"You can tell me anything, you know. I'm friends with Detective LaPorte, and he and I work together sometimes."

That seemed to reassure her, and her face perked up a bit. "I had to give a statement to the police last night. The police! They think I had something to do with Charlotte Devereaux's death."

"That's what I heard. Detective LaPorte told me you fought with her on New Year's Eve and someone reported it."

"It's true. We both went to Odilia LaPorte's restaurant. I only wanted to use the ladies' restroom, but then we ran into each other." She frowned, as if the moment still bothered her. "How was I supposed to know we both picked the same restaurant?"

"What did you two talk about?" It was hard to picture the grandmother beside me in a screaming match with Charlotte Devereaux, since the woman was half her age and twice her size.

"That's the thing. We weren't really that loud. It was a private conversation. I didn't mean to start something, but I couldn't help myself when I saw her."

She hadn't answered my question, so I tried again. "Were you two arguing about her new business? Is that what set you off?"

"Partly." She crossed her arms. "I told her she shouldn't have made all those plans to expand without talking to the rest of us first. We're like family down here. Everyone knows that. We work together. It's how we've always done things. But then Charlotte went and blindsided us."

Amazing to think we'd both attended the wedding planners' meeting only a day before, when Paxton announced all of the changes Charlotte planned to make. "That was some meeting, all right."

"He didn't even mention the worst part. She'd already up and hired a baker to run her cake business. Someone from Commander's Palace over in New Orleans. I worked right across the hall from her. Now, why would she do that?"

"I don't know. But you've got a great reputation. What difference could one more bakery make?"

Bettina grudgingly uncrossed her arms. "Wait 'til you've been in business as long as I have. This is how it starts: Someone new comes in and then they drop their prices, so people get used to paying only half what these cakes are really worth. Before long, she'd put us right out of business. Mark my words . . . it was only a matter of time."

I eyed her. *Surely she's exaggerating.* Everyone knew about Pink Cake Boxes. People waited three weeks for an appointment during the wedding season, for goodness sakes. She also got more press in bridal magazines than anyone else on the Great River Road. "But what about all those magazine articles you've been in? They must bring you tons of publicity. Enough to set you up for life."

She scoffed. "You'd be surprised. Most times people just tear out the pictures of my cakes and bring them to their own bakers. It's not right, but it's what they do. I'm not complaining, mind you, because my family gets a kick out of seeing me in those magazines. But I've never made a lot of money off them."

I leaned back. And here I thought Bettina's business was bulletproof. Little did I know the publicity didn't necessarily translate into more sales. No wonder she was so angry with Charlotte. "You said you talked to Charlotte about other things that night. What else was bothering you?"

"Well, I found out—"

"Excuse me." It was Trudi again, who'd returned to the bakery in a huff. She stood in the doorway with her hands clasped in front of her. "Have you seen my gloves? I must've dropped them here." She quickly scanned the carpet, all but ignoring the two of us.

"No, I haven't seen them," I said. "But, look . . . Bettina's back."

"Sorry I took so long." Bettina glanced at her sheepishly. "I was trying to find the sketch you wanted."

"Don't worry 'bout it. You can show it to my wedding planner. Aha!" She lunged forward and disappeared under our table. A moment later, she reemerged with the gloves in her hand. "I knew it!"

"But I've got the drawing now." Bettina's voice was hopeful. "Look, it's right over there, on top of that case. Would you like to see it?"

"I said that won't be necessary. You can call my wedding planner today. She'll work out the details with you."

Once she jammed the gloves on her hands, Trudi turned and stalked away again. It took a moment for the air to recover after her whirlwind appearance.

"Guess she put me in my place." Bettina sighed and lumbered to her feet. "I'd better set up a meeting with her wedding planner. I heard she's using Suzi Wan now."

I wanted to say something comforting; I really did. But between her obvious resignation and Trudi's rudeness, nothing came to mind. So I rose too and walked to the door. "Hang in there. Detective La-Porte will nab a suspect soon. Then things will get back to normal."

She didn't look convinced. "I wish I could believe you. I really do. But I don't think that's ever going to happen."

Chapter 15

B ettina left the bakery through the same side door she'd used earlier. She didn't even bother to retrieve the sketch pad she'd placed on the display case.

No wonder Lance considers her a person of interest. She didn't defend herself very well, and, if her current state of mind was any indication, she felt guilty about something.

Maybe it was best to leave the building once and for all. So far, I'd run into more people on this side of the Factory—including Suzi, Hank, Trudi, and Bettina—than I ever thought possible, and our conversations left me more confused than ever. By now, the words jumbled together like an alphabet soup of people, places, and information.

Not only that, but the barista downstairs must've skimped on the caffeine in my mocha, because my brain still felt like mush.

So, I left the bakery and headed for the elevator, which I guessed would be waiting for me at the end of the hall. *No such luck.* Instead of the *pppiiinnnggg* of it coming to greet me, I heard a different sound altogether: a methodical *cccrrruuunnncchh* as metal gears chewed through paper.

The noise seemed to be coming from Happily Ever After Events, across the hall. Sure enough, when I stepped over to the other wall, the sound grew louder.

Curious now, I glanced over my shoulder, just to be safe, and cautiously pushed open the door with the faux-painted roses above it. *What's another minute or two in the grand scheme of things?* True, I still had to call Lance, but the noise was irresistible.

I stepped into the offices of the special events company, where I once more saw sweet paintings done in pastel colors: roses trellised across the wall and grassy hills tapered to a far-off horizon, and a quaint Dutch door stood half-open. The whimsical colors didn't quite match the sound that arose behind it. *Cccrrruuunnnccchhh.*

I carefully pushed open the painted door and spied Paxton in his office. He stood with his shoulders angled to the hall and his hand outstretched, only inches from a black plastic box.

It was a paper shredder, of all things. He carefully fed one sheet into it, and then another, while I watched. Each time he forced the page through the opening, as if he thought the machine might spit it out again.

Why, I'd know the logo at the top of the sheets anywhere. It was the red, white, and blue banner for Southern Louisiana Bank and Trust, which was my bank too.

Without warning, Paxton suddenly glanced up. "Missy?" The *cccrrruuunnnccchhh* abruptly stopped. "What're you doing here?" It was an accusation, not a question, and we both knew it.

"Sorry if I startled you." I drew closer, willing the shakiness from my voice. What was Paxton Haney doing with a paper shredder and his bank statements? It didn't seem logical. "I heard a noise in here. Since you guys always opened up at ten, I wanted to make sure everything was all right."

"That so? You heard a noise all the way up the stairs and down the hall? Your ears must be amazing."

"No, of course not." I tried to sound nonchalant. "I had business up here, in Bettina's bakery. And you know how thin the walls are. They're like paper."

We lapsed into an awkward silence. It seemed like neither of us felt inclined to tell the truth at the moment. Maybe if I engaged in some chitchat, I could take the edge off.

"It's been a rough morning." I tried to appear casual as I leaned against the doorframe. "Did you know someone smashed in my French door? Hacked the stuffing clean out of it. I hope you have a burglar alarm in here. I'd hate for something like that to happen to you."

It seemed to work, since he moved over to an armchair he'd placed behind the desk. "That's terrible. Did you call the police?"

"I did. They dusted for fingerprints. The crook bashed it twelve ways to Sunday, so it's a total loss. But at least nothing was taken."

"That's good." He placed a bank statement on his desk—face-down, of course–while he took the chair. "Guess you can't be too careful these days. Though I don't know what they expected to find in a hat studio."

"Tell me about it. It's not like I keep a safe in there or anything." He casually indicated the paperwork around him. "Look, I've got a million things to do. And it sounds like you're busy this morning too. Maybe we can catch up later."

It's time to bring out the big guns. "Sure. By the way, you'll never guess who I ran into downstairs. Hank Dupre, of all people."

That did it.

Paxton blinked; a tiny crack in his smooth façade. He could talk his way out of my questions, but he couldn't hide such an automatic reaction. "You don't say."

"Yep. And he mentioned you were thinking of selling your business. Which I couldn't believe, since you were just talking about Charlotte's plans to expand it. During the meeting yesterday, remember?"

"Of course I do. That's what Charlotte planned to do before she died."

So he didn't try to hide the fact he met with a Realtor this morning. But why would he schedule an appointment with Hank Dupre at dawn, when no one else would see them? That alone seemed suspicious enough.

"I never thought you'd sell. Your speech made it sound like y'all had big plans to expand."

"Yeah, well, like I said . . . we did. But to tell you the truth, I never wanted to add all that other stuff. Not now." He blinked again. "In fact, I wanted to retire. I'm almost sixty. The way I figure it, I have ten or twenty good years left to do what *I* want to do."

"Did you ever tell Charlotte how you felt?" I leaned forward, even more curious now. Why wouldn't he confide in his cousin if he wanted to retire? Family was family, after all. Surely she'd understand. "Maybe she would've bought out your half. Then you could've done whatever you wanted."

"You don't know how hard I tried." He leaned forward too, as if he'd been waiting for someone like me to bring it up. "Charlotte wouldn't let me retire. She said she needed me, because I handled the finances."

"But she handled all the clients. Right?"

"That's the easy part, to tell you the truth. Everyone thinks this business is *soooo* glamorous. Gourmet food . . . ritzy mansions . . . newspaper photographers. What's not to like?" He thumped the desk, and the paper jumped. "I'll tell you what's not to like. Everything's all fun and games until the dance floor clears. Do you know what it's like to collect money from these people?"

I managed to nod, although his sudden outburst surprised me.

"It's like pulling teeth, Miss DuBois. Like our clients have amnesia the minute the music stops. That's when they suddenly realize they have to pay for it all."

"But Charlotte seemed to enjoy it so very much. We always had a wonderful time when we worked together."

He rolled his eyes. "Of course *she* did. I told you: She had the easy part. Meet with clients, plan menus, that kind of thing." Now he smoothed the paper flat, as if to erase his outburst. "Lord knows I tried to get my point across. Several times. She wouldn't hear of it. Said we're family, and family sticks together. She worried what people would do if we split up the company. She said they'd smell trouble."

My thoughts immediately rewound to a conversation down the hall, only a little while ago. Trudi Whidbee sat in a chair next to me in Pink Cake Boxes and glibly announced she'd fired Happily Ever After Events. She mentioned it in passing, like an afterthought.

"Trudi Whidbee told me she canceled her contract with you. She said she picked a brand-new wedding planner."

Paxton continued to smooth the sheet. "Yeah, well. She's not the only one. Clients have been calling all day, every day, since Charlotte died. That's why I've got to sell now. Pretty soon, there won't be any contracts left."

I watched him palm the paper, until my gaze wandered to the filing cabinet behind him. Last night, the cabinet's drawers bulged with manila folders; too many for them to close. Now, the drawers lay flush with the cabinet's face, which meant he must've emptied them overnight.

"That's too bad." I returned my gaze to his face. "I'm sorry people are reacting like that."

"That's just part of it. Charlotte's plans upset a lot of the shop owners around here. I know that. Everyone thinks Charlotte wanted to put them out of business. Someone even threatened me."

Another memory came crashing back. This one involved a conversation I overheard on the steps at Morningside Planation.

The day dawned cold and gray. Dana LeBoeuf wore a flowered skirt and combat boots, didn't she? And Bettina wore the tight ballerina bun, like always.

The two women whispered urgently on the stairs, while I did my best to sink into the wall behind the door. Dana sounded downright calm compared to Bettina, almost content. Especially when she mentioned she had "taken care" of a problem. *What did she mean by that?*

"Look, I really have to get back to work, Miss DuBois." His voice broke through my reverie. "Good luck to you, Mr. Haney. I hope everything works out for you in the next few days."

"All I know is things are moving way too fast. One day we're going to expand the company, and the next day I have to sell it. Who would've thought things would turn out like this?"

Who, indeed. I didn't reply to his question, although I couldn't agree with him more.

By the time I made my way downstairs, the first wave of guilt washed over me. I was supposed to be gone only a few minutes; long enough to grab a *venti* mocha from the Starbucks in the lobby. Somehow, though, that simple errand morphed into myriad conversations with people like Paxton Haney, Bettina Leblanc, and Hank Dupre.

Ambrose must be worried sick about me by now. I quickly reached into the pocket of the skirt, ready to whisk out my phone, but felt only fabric and air. *How could I forget again?* I'd left the cell on the counter in his studio.

My only choice was to hurry back. Once I put his mind at ease, I'd give Lance a call and report on my comings and goings. Although he'd been reluctant to include me in Charlotte's murder investigation—then again, when *wasn't* he reluctant—he'd surely be interested in my most recent discoveries.

Truth be told, I had more access to the folks who worked around Charlotte on a daily basis than *he* did. Plus, I had an excellent motive for wanting to find her killer: to bring brides back to my studio and clear my name. That was why my questions wouldn't seem out of place and why people might be more willing to answer them.

I rode the elevator to the first floor and then hurried across the lobby. Thankfully, the skies outside looked clear now and the windows rain-free.

Once I exited the building, I noticed smashed crabgrass on the concrete medians, slick puddles that pockmarked the asphalt like moon craters, and willow branches bent sideways, their limbs slack.

I resumed my trek to the right, lost in thought. So much had happened since I first drove into the parking lot at the Factory that morning. Too much to absorb.

After a moment, something sounded behind me. An engine sputtered and coughed as a car drew near. I gave it a wide berth by edging closer to the building.

The sputtering grew louder as the car pulled up beside me. In the next instant, something wet and cold splattered against my leg. I reared back on the kitten heels, but it was too late: oily water from a nearby puddle splashed across my skirt like dishwater slopping onto a sponge.

The stain quickly seeped sideways and down the front. I was about to yelp when the owner of the car slammed on the brakes and jerked to a stop.

It was a forest green Volvo with a missing taillight. The car suddenly reversed course and inched back to me in fits and starts.

Once we were side-by-side again, the driver burst out of the car. It was Prudence Fortenberry, of all people, wearing that ridiculous faux-fur hat again.

She hustled around the hood of her car and joined me on the sidewalk. "I'm so sorry! I didn't see you standing there." She huffed the words, clearly out of breath.

"Hello, Prudence." I struggled to sound even-keeled. How could I possibly return the skirt to Ambrose now? Dirty water splattered my left side, from knee to hem. Not to mention some overspray fanned across the front.

"Let me take care of that for you." Prudence awkwardly reached for the Volvo's passenger door with her left hand, since her right was still bandaged. After wrenching open the door, she leaned into the car and began to rummage around the front seat.

She didn't have much room to work with. She'd shoved a red Samsonite suitcase on the passenger's side and a burlap book bag directly under it, on the floorboard. The bag overflowed with sheet music bound in goldenrod covers.

"Really," I said, "don't worry about it. You didn't mean to splash me."

She gave the suitcase a final shove, obviously deaf to my protests. "Now where did I put my purse?" she mumbled.

"I said it's okay." I sank back on my heels, the taffeta skirt sticking to my calf like a wet paper towel. "It was an accident. That's all."

"But I insist." She gave up on the front seat and leaned over to inspect the back. "You *must* let me pay for dry cleaning."

I peeked over her shoulder as she contemplated the paraphernalia in the backseat: another red suitcase—apparently it was a matched set—more sheet music in burlap book bags and a pile of shoes on the floorboard.

"Are you going somewhere?" My guess was an out-of-town wedding, what with the piano music and all.

"Hmmm?" She continued to rummage through the backseat with her left hand. "Here we go." She finally located the wayward purse under a pair of shoes. "How much do you think the dry cleaner will charge?"

"You *really* don't have to do that." Even though she'd messed up my skirt, her apology sounded sincere enough.

"No, I insist." She opened the flap of her handbag and winced as she pulled out a ten-dollar bill with her injured hand.

"By the way . . . whatever happened to your hand?" I watched her carefully extract the bill. It was hard not to stare, since the pink bandage looked like a flesh-colored mitten.

She shrugged. "Just a little mishap. Nothing serious. I should be fine in a week or two."

"So you don't have a wedding gig this weekend, then."

She thrust the bill at me, clearly in a hurry. "What?"

"I thought maybe you were going to a wedding." I nodded at the paraphernalia. "You know, the luggage."

Come to think of it, two suitcases *was* a bit excessive. Most weddings lasted six hours or so, and that was for both the ceremony and reception. But Prudence had enough clothes and music for ten times that amount in her car.

"Uh, yeah," she said. "I'd love to stay and talk, but I'm kind of in a hurry." She flipped the pocketbook closed. "Nice to see you. And I'm so sorry about the skirt."

She skittered away before I could reply. Once she reached the driver's side, she jerked on the door handle and slid into the car, all business now.

The last thing I noticed was the missing taillight as she pulled away from the curb.

The puckering of taffeta against my leg reminded me of my predicament. While Prudence had given me money to clean it, I hated to have Ambrose see me like this. Maybe I should tuck the folds in close to make the stain less obvious when I got back to his studio.

It's worth a shot. So, I set off across the parking lot again, and even hopscotched over a few more puddles, although the damage was already done. The minute I came within spitting distance of Ambrose's Allure Couture, I grabbed the wet fabric in my fist and prepared to sidestep into his studio.

But something caught my eye first. A fresh piece of plywood leaned against the wall of my studio next door. Not only that, but someone had swept the welcome mat clean and even rinsed off the ground around it.

I hurried into Ambrose's studio with my mouth open, forgetting all about my earlier plan to sneak in sideways. "Ambrose!"

He stood across the way, by the three-way mirror, and he frowned when I entered. "Hey . . . I was about to come get you. Where've you been?"

"I'm so sorry." I rushed to his side and gave him a quick hug. "But I left my cell on your counter, so I couldn't call you. Thank you for fixing my door! And you'll never guess who-all I've talked to."

I led him to the counter, the ruined skirt all but forgotten, and slid onto one of the bar stools. Once he took the other stool, I launched into a quick rundown of my conversations with Hank, Paxton, Bettina, and the rest. I spent most of my breath on Paxton and his shredded bank statements.

"That *does* seem strange," he said, when I'd finished. "You need to tell your detective friend about it. There's no reason for Paxton to destroy bank records like that. At least, no normal reason."

"I agree." I leaned forward to grab my cell, which wasn't easy considering wet taffeta weighed me down. "By the way . . . I kinda got your skirt wet. I'm so sorry. I'll go to the dry cleaners just as soon as I have a chance to call Lance."

"Don't worry about that. I'm only glad you made it back safe and sound."

I threw him another smile, and then I rose and headed for the chifforobe that leaned against the far wall of his studio. Once I'd retrieved my corduroys, I quickly moved to the dressing room and changed, and then I tucked the ruined skirt under my arm and rejoined him at the counter.

Ambrose glanced up from his cell as I approached. "By the way, one of my clients just texted. She'll be here in five minutes."

I squinted, since I couldn't quite remember if he'd told me his schedule for the day. "Which client?"

"The redhead, from yesterday. We never got to finish."

"Oh, *that* client." The Victoria's Secret model. The one who seemed as wary of me as I was of her. "I don't like the way she looked at you."

"She didn't look at me. You're crazy."

He said it in jest, but the hairs on the back of my neck bristled anyway. "Just be careful around that one. She looked like she wanted to eat you up for lunch."

Ambrose chuckled, clearly not seeing the danger in the situation. "Okay. Now we're down to four minutes."

"I'm going. I'm going."

"Maybe you should grab some breakfast when you meet up with Lance. Knowing you, you forgot to eat anything this morning."

"Me? You're the one who looked ready to faint yesterday." Come to think of it, though, getting a quick bite to eat might not be such a bad idea, since a dull rumble worked its way through my belly. "I'll call Lance and see what he says. Then you can have your precious studio all to yourself."

Ambrose slowly lowered the phone. "Thank you. And you don't have anything to worry about. I just want to finish that girl's dress and get paid."

"Gotcha. Want me to grab you anything to eat while I'm out and about?"

"Sure. How 'bout a breakfast sandwich and a smoothie. You know what I like."

For some reason, that tickled me. "You bet I do."

Chapter 16

Once I left Ambrose's Allure Couture—rather reluctantly, I might add—I returned to the parking lot, brought out my cell and dialed Lance's number. He answered right away, which was becoming a habit with him.

"Hey, Missy. What's up?"

"Hi, Lance. I've got so much to tell you." Come to think of it, that was an understatement. "You're not gonna believe what I found out after you left me this morning. Can you meet me at your mom's place for some breakfast?"

His mother owned Miss Odilia's Southern Eatery, which was one of the newest and most popular restaurants in Bleu Bayou. Everyone loved his mom's biscuits and gravy, not to mention her fried chicken and waffles.

He inhaled sharply. "I don't know. I'm snowed under with the investigation. Can it wait?"

"Probably not. It's about Charlotte's murder."

"Okay, then. I'll make a few calls and I'll head over to my mom's."

Even though it was only nine in the morning, my mouth watered at the thought of Mrs. LaPorte's fried chicken. I considered that as I headed for my convertible.

By now, the entire parking lot was full, so I carefully backed out of my space when I reached Ringo, and then I turned onto the surface road that would take me to Miss Odilia's Southern Eatery. Thank goodness the restaurant was close by, because otherwise I'd have to pass some of the town's other landmarks, like Dippin' Donuts, which Grady owned.

Grady. Even the thought of passing by his doughnut shop now took my breath away.

Yesterday, when he asked me out to dinner, I happily accepted. But that was then. That was before Ambrose propped me up this morning as we surveyed my ruined door. He seemed more upset about the crime than I was; as if the assault happened to him and not me.

Not only that, but then he arranged to fix the damage and even cleaned off my front stoop for good measure. How could I betray him like this? I felt horrible, and I hadn't even done anything wrong yet.

Lost in thought, I almost missed the entrance to Miss Odilia's parking lot. A quick twist of the wrist corrected that, and I pulled up alongside Lance's grimy Oldsmobile in the first row. One day I'd convince him to visit Sparkle N' Shine for a full-service car wash, but not today. Today, we had other, more important things to discuss.

I parked the car and hopped out, and that's when I spied Lance waiting for me by the front door, a thick notebook in his hand.

"Hey, there," he called out, as soon as I approached him.

"Hi, Lance. Thanks for meeting me."

"This is the second time today I've seen you. People are gonna talk."

"Don't start up with me. You have no idea where I've been."

I led him into the restaurant and over to the hostess stand. Unlike later in the day, when a line of customers would wind from the stand to the parking lot, only a few people milled around this early in the morning.

The restaurant began its life as a 1930s bungalow. While Odilia LaPorte replaced most of the plumbing and electrical fixtures when she converted it to a restaurant, she left other details alone, like the old Baldwin piano in the front room and an oil painting of the original owners on the fireplace mantle. Even the crossbeams in the dining room were original, including ones that teepeed over a certain table where Ambrose and I had dined.

A freckle-faced hostess led us to a different table now.

"Thank you," Lance told her, as he pulled out a chair for me.

"Would you like some coffee?" She set two paper coasters on the table in front of us.

"Please," I said. "I'll take mine black, and Lance here likes his with cream."

"Yes, ma'am. Zach will be your server today."

Lance tossed his notebook on the table as she walked away. He chose the chair next to mine and settled into it. "So, what's all this about?"

"I found out some new things with Charlotte's death." I glanced at the notebook and spied her name and the date she died on its cover.

"What's that?"

"This? It's my murder book. I use it to record everything about the investigation."

"Everything?" Although I'd discovered Charlotte's body only two days ago, the book already bulged with bits of paper and neon sticky notes.

"Yep. We're talking witness statements, preliminary autopsy results, crime-scene photos. You name it—it's all in there."

I touched the cover, which was cool and nubby. "That must be helpful. Otherwise, how would you keep all those teeny-tiny details straight?"

He gave a raspy chuckle. "Those 'teeny-tiny details,' as you put it, are what's gonna solve this crime. My job is to figure out which ones are important and which ones aren't." He shrugged, as if he was talking about how to solve the Sunday crossword puzzle and not a murder, for goodness sakes.

"Where do you even start?"

"I do a timeline first. It helps me keep the chronology straight. That way, if people come back and try to change their location, I know they're lying."

"See . . . that's what would kill me. I'd hate to think people would lie to my face. Do you ever get used to it?"

"Not really. But it doesn't bother me as much as it used to. I've seen what happens when people lie to a cop. It eats away at them. It might take a while, but eventually they'll come back and tell me what they really saw."

I thought about that for a moment. "But couldn't that take years? By then a case would be cold. At least, that's what they say on TV."

He shook his head. "Don't believe everything you see on those shows. There's no such thing as a 'cold case.' Not as long as there's a cop who has a murder book like this. As a matter of fact . . ." He flipped it open to reveal a sketch of what looked like a parking lot, with wheel stops, dotted lines, and a caution sign. "I'm going to re-create the crime later today. Go over the position of the whiskey barrel, the victim's body . . . that kind of thing."

Just then, Odilia LaPorte, who wore a chef's coat, appeared at our table, and Lance quickly flipped the book closed. Odilia wore a snowy chignon, like always, which she'd tucked under a black hairnet. Her round face split in two the moment she spied her son.

"Shut my mouth and call me Shirley!" She swallowed Lance in a bear hug. "My hostess told me you were here."

"Hey, Mom." Lance threw me a sheepish grin. "Don't forget about Missy."

She turned and wrapped her arms around me next, the smells of cooking oil, fried bread crumbs, and fresh garlic wafting up from her coat.

"Hello, Mrs. LaPorte."

She immediately released me. "How many times do I have to ask you to call me Odilia? Gah-lee, you're making me feel as old as dirt."

"Sorry, Miss Odilia. No disrespect intended. It's just how I was raised."

"I understand that." She clucked her tongue. "Now, what brings you two into my little restaurant? And there's only one right answer, you know."

"Why, the food, of course." I feigned innocence. "Why else would we come?"

"Good girl."

"But we also have a lot to discuss," Lance said.

Leave it to him to steamroll right over the pleasantries and get down to business. No wonder Lance made such a good cop.

"That right?" Odilia said. "What're you working on?"

"Missy here is helping me with the Charlotte Devereaux investigation. She's the one who found the body, you know."

"I heard about that." Odilia clucked her tongue again. "Terrible tragedy. Just awful. And especially since I saw Charlotte the other night."

I quickly eyed the empty chair across the way. Odds were good Odilia would say no, but it couldn't hurt to offer it. "Can you join us for a few minutes? Lance here told me Charlotte came to your restaurant on New Year's Eve."

She glanced around the dining room, which was only half full, before pulling out the chair and sitting down. "Guess a few minutes won't hurt." The cooking smells reemerged as she settled into it. "We don't get crowded until lunchtime. But I already told Lance what I saw that night."

"You did," he said. "Apparently the victim met up with Bettina Leblanc in the hallway, by the kitchen."

"Um, hm. I could hear the two of them fussin' from clear across the room. You know it's bad when you can hear something over the grease cookin'."

"But wasn't the whole restaurant loud that night?" I asked. "I imagine you were packed, it being New Year's Eve."

"Well, it wasn't quiet," she admitted. "But those two caught my ear. I had to leave my stove just to see what all the fuss was about."

Bits and pieces of my earlier conversation with Lance bubbled up now. Apparently, Bettina blamed the dustup on too much alcohol, although the coroner's report didn't agree with her.

Odilia pointed to a spot over Lance's shoulder. "The two of 'em got into it right over there, in that hallway. That's one of the most public places 'round here you can fight with someone."

I nodded, even though I wished the fight would've happened in the dining room where we sat, since a video camera captured everything that took place here. "I'm sure you told Lance what you know, but I still think it's strange Bettina blamed their fight on too much wine."

"Well, she was half right." Odilia glanced from me to Lance. "I told you about that, son. Bettina was drunker than a skunk. Almost thought she was gonna topple right over onto the floor when I came outta my kitchen to shush 'em."

"But what about Charlotte?" I asked. "Was she sober?"

"As a judge." Odilia pursed his lips now. "I think that was part of the problem. When Bettina started laying into her, Charlotte didn't have much choice but to hear her out. She looked afraid of Bettina, to tell you the truth."

"What were they fighting about?" Although I didn't want to hog the conversation, Lance had heard most of this before, while I hadn't. And I couldn't understand why two women would fight in one of the town's most popular restaurants, and on its busiest night of the year.

"Well, I've been thinking about that," Odilia said. "At first I thought it was about business. You know, since they both worked around here. I figured maybe one of 'em bad-mouthed the other to a client."

As Odilia spoke, Lance slowly edged the notebook away from his elbow, flipped it open, and withdrew a Bic from the book's spine, all nonchalance. "You've changed your mind about that, Mom? Sounds like you don't think the argument was about work, after all."

"I *have* changed my mind. I was gonna call you about it when I had a chance." A cloud passed over Odilia's face. "I think it was more personal than that. Bettina didn't like something Charlotte had done. She wagged her finger at her so much, I thought for sure it was gonna fly right off her hand."

"Interesting." Lance scribbled something or other into his notebook. "Did you hear the actual words?"

"Not really. I could barely understand Bettina. She's a sloppy drunk, you know."

Lance's pen stalled. "Anything else?"

"Just what I already told you. Bettina wanted her to make amends for something. Said it was the Christian thing to do. Her face got all red and puffy when she said that."

I was about to pose another question when a figure appeared behind Lance's shoulder. It was the hostess, who'd returned with our coffees.

"Here you go," she said. "I'm sorry it took me so long." Apparently, she didn't expect to see Odilia at our table, because she almost dropped the cups when she noticed her boss. "The pot was empty and I couldn't find the filters. I'll run back and get you some cream."

The girl somehow managed to right the cups and set them on the table before she hurried away.

"Well, guess it's time for me to get back to the kitchen." Odilia pushed her chair back and rose. "Those filters are right on top of the shelf, plain as day. I swaney, sometimes I wonder how we get anything done around here."

Once she moved away from our table, I turned to Lance. "Was any of that news to you?"

"Only the part about her changing her mind. And that's the first time she said anything about making amends."

"Seems like she just remembered that part." I took a sip of coffee, which was hot and strong, just like my earlier cup at the Starbucks kiosk. "I'm sure she had a lot going on in her kitchen that night. I'm surprised she caught as much as she did."

"My mom's a good witness. She doesn't miss a trick. Maybe because she had to put up with me for so long."

I chuckled. "Good point. You definitely kept her on her toes."

"Now . . . where were we?" He leaned back and lifted his mug. "You said something about new details. Start at the beginning and tell me everything."

Once I'd told Lance about my conversations at the Factory—especially my time with Paxton Haney and his paper shredder—our meal drew to a close.

By now, he'd written more notes in his murder book, and I'd polished off a full plate of chicken and waffles.

"I'm stuffed as a tick." I pushed the plate away. "That's what my grandpa would say."

Lance did the same. "No, that's not right. He'd say 'stuffed as a tick on a hound dog.' Every one of your grandpa's sayings had a hound dog in it."

I grinned. "Whaddya know. You actually paid attention to him all those times you came around to my house."

"Didn't think I had much of a choice. Look, this has been great and all, but I've gotta get back to the police station. I told the medical examiner I'd call him at ten, and we're past that now." He scooped up his notebook and rose.

I began to get ready to leave, but he motioned for me to stay put.

"No . . . don't get up on my account. You still have some coffee left. And don't even think about trying to pay the bill. My mom won't let either of us do that."

"At least let me leave a tip." I started to reach for some bills in my pocket, but he beat me to the punch and tossed five dollars on the table.

"That should do it," he said. "I'll call you later, especially if the ME tells me anything new."

He swung the notebook to his side and began to walk away. Once he disappeared, I pulled out my cell to check the time. The screen showed three new texts. One was from Ambrose, who asked for a breakfast burrito instead of a sandwich. The second was from Beatrice, who wrote something about another bride canceling her appointment.

Ouch. Just when I thought things were beginning to settle down, it looked like my clients still didn't trust me. Why else would a bride up and cancel like that?

I numbly reached for the coffee cup. Guess I had no choice but to do damage control once I returned to the Factory. At this rate, I'd never be able to pay my bills, and I needed every single penny in January to make up for the holidays. It was the only way I could keep the lights on, the storeroom supplied, and Beatrice's paychecks coming until the wedding season kicked in again.

I debated calling Beatrice right then and there. Maybe we could put our heads together and figure out a way to stop the downward spiral.

Before I could do that, though, the last message on the screen caught my eye.

Someone had texted only a few minutes before. Unlike the first two messages, this one was preceded by the words *No Caller ID.* How strange. My cell always gave the person's name, or, if not a name, at least a telephone number.

But this person had deliberately blocked the information. The message they sent was brief:

Did you like your door? Hope you learned a lesson. We all know CD wasn't worth spit.

My fingers gripped the coffee cup's handle. The text was only three sentences long. Really just a scattering of vowels and consonants. But the tone . . . I could almost hear someone crow in the background.

After an eternity, I dredged my gaze away from it. Everything around me seemed so normal. A couple of businesswomen sat at the next table over, their perfectly coiffed heads bent together. Across from them was a mom and her toddler, who faced a giant pile of Cheerios on the tray of his high chair. Even farther back stood the hostess, who twirled a strand of hair while she surveyed the dining room.

Just another normal breakfast at Miss Odilia's Southern Eatery. I reluctantly returned my gaze to the phone, unable to resist the pull of it. Obviously, *CD* stood for Charlotte Devereaux. But why would someone tell me she wasn't "worth spit"? And why was I being punished for something?

If only Lance hadn't left already. He'd know what to do.

Speaking of which . . . am I being watched? Lance always told me about thugs who liked to hang around afterward to watch their victim's faces. Was my texter sitting somewhere nearby, hoping to see the startled look on my face?

I pushed the coffee cup away and wobbled to my feet. The industrial carpet blurred underneath as I dashed through the dining room with the cell phone in my hand.

I moved on autopilot all the way to the parking lot. There wasn't time to think; time to do much of anything but breathe . . . and even that wasn't easy. I scrambled over to Ringo and hopped in, and then I instinctively pointed the car toward the Factory. Since Lance was tied up with the medical examiner, I needed to find Ambrose. He'd help me make sense of the message.

Chapter 17

Nothing registered as I drove away from the restaurant and pulled onto the feeder road. At one point someone honked—at least I thought it was intended for me—but the sound was muffled, vague. I didn't notice anything else until I arrived at the Factory and pulled into a parking space directly in front of my studio.

Someone was already there. It was a woman, who'd curled her finger around an edge of the plywood and pulled it back a bit. There was no mistaking the teal Chanel suit. Why-ever would Suzi Wan want to peek inside my empty studio?

I practically fell out of the car and moved over to her. "Excuse me. Can I help you?"

She startled and the plywood snapped back into place. "Missy ... you scared me to death! You shouldn't go around sneaking up on people like that. It's not polite."

Polite? By all rights, she stood in front of *my* studio, inspecting *my* property, but I was supposed to apologize? "I'm not sneaking around. You're standing on my welcome mat."

"What?" Her gaze fell to the ground. "So I am. Silly me. And it's such a lovely mat too. Wherever did you find it?"

I glanced at the plain rush mat, which was faded and frayed. *Talk about changing the subject.* "Homestyle Hardware. Is there something I can do for you?"

"I only wanted to see what happened to your studio, since you told me about it this morning."

"Yes, well ... There's nothing much to see. Ambrose cleaned up the mess."

"I thought I'd stop by and take a peek anyway, since I got called back for a client meeting. Unfortunately, it's a new client and she's very high maintenance."

Her mention of a new client reminded me of something. Hadn't Trudi Whidbee casually announced she'd hired Suzi to plan her wedding? She'd tossed off the comment as if it meant nothing to her. "By the way, I ran into Trudi Whidbee this morning. She told me she hired you as her new wedding planner."

"She did, did she? Then I guess it's not a secret." Suzi laughed, but it was brittle. "You know what they say about small towns: News around here travels at the speed of boredom."

"Yes, that's what they say. But I was surprised everything happened so fast between you two. Charlotte only died a few days ago."

The color slowly drained from her face. "Well, I don't know what the Whidbee girl was thinking. I can't speak for her. And I happened to have some free time."

"Really?" Only this morning, Suzi claimed to be booked solid. Before I could question her, she suddenly reached for my wrist.

"Can I ask you something? What do you think's going on around here? Seems like the whole town is going crazy." She had a remarkably strong grip for a woman her age. "You need to be careful. I have a feeling it's not over yet."

"Excuse me?"

Her words were odd, but it was her face that startled me. She looked haunted, as if she knew something I didn't.

"Look, Suzi. If you know what's going on around here, you need to tell Lance LaPorte. He's the one investigating Charlotte's murder."

That snapped her out of her reverie, and she quickly dropped my wrist. "My goodness . . . what was I thinking? Don't pay any attention to me. Of course I don't know anything else about it. I'm just on edge. Guess I'll see you later."

She rushed away before I could say more. In an instant, she'd moved past Ambrose's studio and started up the path that would take her to the atrium. She never once glanced back.

If that doesn't beat all. Once she disappeared into the lobby, I massaged my wrist as I walked into Ambrose's Allure Couture. Hallelujah, Bo was by the counter again.

He grinned the minute I entered. "Hey, there."

"Thank goodness you're here, Bo."

"Uh, Missy." His smile quickly faded. "Did you forget some-thing?"

"What? I don't think so."

"The breakfast burrito, remember? You were going to bring me something to eat. Don't tell me you forgot all about it."

My heart sank. "Oh, shine! I *did* forget." It was a wonder Bo didn't disown me right then and there. Everything I did for him lately turned out wrong. "I'll go back and get it for you. It won't take me long."

I began to move, but he stopped me. "No, it's okay. Don't worry about it. I can hold out until lunch. Besides, you look like some-thing's bothering you."

Only Bo could read my mood in three seconds flat. At this point, I didn't know whether that made me feel better, or worse.

"I have a lot on my mind." I reached into the pocket where I kept my cell. "Here. Read this."

His eyes flew over the screen once I handed him the phone. "When you did get this?"

"Maybe ten minutes ago. It happened right after Lance and I ate breakfast at his mom's place. Who do you think sent it?"

He handed it back to me. "I have no idea. But that's evidence. You need to show it to Lance. Maybe he can trace it."

"Maybe." I carefully set the device on the counter, reluctant to handle it any more than necessary. "But it looks like they blocked the call."

"Yeah, but maybe someone in his department can still trace it. That's an admission of guilt."

"What I can't get over is the tone. Like they're blaming Charlotte for her own death. That part creeps me out more than anything."

"I agree." He draped his arm around my shoulders protectively. "That's not something a sane person would write. Good thing we're in the same rent house so I get to keep an eye on you at night."

My heart sank even more. I wouldn't be home tonight for Am-brose to protect me. Tonight I'd be on a date with Grady. *What a wonderful way to repay his concern.* I burrowed my head into his chest, grateful for the camouflage.

"I'll tell you what." Too soon, he pulled away. "Why don't you give me your phone and I'll take it to the police station for you. I lied when I said I could hold out until lunch. I'm starving."

"Really? You'd do that for me?"

"Of course."

I reached for the phone, until I remembered something else. "I might have to use it first, though. Beatrice told me about another bride who wants to cancel her appointment. At this rate, I won't have any clients left by the end of the week."

He scooped up the phone anyway. "That's okay . . . you can use my landline. There's no point in letting your business go down the drain. I'll take this right over to the police station, and then I'll stop at the doughnut store on my way back."

My heart finished its free fall. Not only did someone send me an eerie text, but now Ambrose and Grady would stand in the same room, at the same time, without me there to chaperone. This was on top of everything else, like the cryptic warning from Suzi Wan and the disappearing client. Forget about bad things happening in threes; in my case, they happened in fours and fives.

"Don't look so glum," he said. "I won't be gone that long."

"I know. Just promise you'll hurry back."

Surprisingly, he smiled. "Are you gonna miss me or your cell phone?"

"You, of course. And, by the way . . . what should I tell your clients if anyone comes looking for you?"

"Just tell 'em I'll be right back. My next appointment isn't due for half an hour. That'll give me plenty of time to get over to the police station and then stop at the doughnut store."

"All right." Odds were good my voice sounded as shaky as I felt. "Hope it all works out."

"Don't forget to lock the door behind me. I've got two phones on the landline: one in the workroom and one out here. You can take your pick."

He slid the cell into his pocket and then moved to the exit. The moment he stepped outside, my shoulders slumped. *This isn't going to end well. Maybe if I race after him—*

The ring of a telephone interrupted my thoughts. The noise was coming from the other side of the wall; the wall that separated my studio from Ambrose's. Obviously, I'd forgotten to forward the studio's calls to Beatrice's apartment. One ring passed and then another, so I yelped and hotfooted it to the door. Once I stood in front of my studio again, I peeled back the plywood panel, just like Suzi had done, and inched through the opening. By now, two more rings had come and gone, so I barreled to the counter and lurched for the telephone.

"Hello?" I panted the greeting.

"Hey, Missy. It's me."

Relief washed over me. "Beatrice . . . I'm so glad you called. You wouldn't believe what's been going on around here. By the way, how did you know I'd be in the studio?"

She chuckled. "I didn't, but I figured your cell would have a dead battery, anyway. And if you weren't by this phone, you'd be next door at Mr. Jackson's, so either way you'd hear it."

Smart girl. "You know me too well. And I got your message this morning. Do you have the bride's number? You know, the girl who wants to cancel her appointment."

"That's what I'm calling you about. She left a message, but I wanted to make sure you got it."

I grabbed a receipt by the cash register and Beatrice rattled off the number. "Got it. Anything else I need to know?"

Before she could respond, a knock sounded on the plywood door. It was a gentle *tap* that quickly escalated to a *smack* when someone backhanded the wood.

"Rats—I've gotta go. Someone's here." I said good-bye to Beatrice and dashed to the plywood door.

Halfway there, a voice called out. "Are you open? *Pllleeeaaassseee* tell me you're open." The speaker sounded upset, as if the fate of the free world hung in the balance.

"Yes, I'm open." I pried the plywood back from the wall to give her a larger opening through which to enter. "C'mon in. Sorry about the mess."

She slid in sideways, dragging a clear garment bag behind her. "Hallelujah and pass the mustard!" She deposited the bag, which turned out to be a dress cover from Belle of the Ball Bridals, in my arms.

"What's all this?" I asked. Something gauzy lay under the plastic. "Is it a veil?"

"Don't you remember me?"

"I'm sorry . . . not off the top of my head." I carefully brought the veil to the counter and slid it out of the wrapping. "This looks like one of mine, though."

"It *is* one of yours. You made it about a year ago. My wedding's this weekend and . . ." Her voice trailed off as we both eyed the pile of lace.

A giant tear zigzagged across the front. My heart sank, since haphazard rips were the hardest kind to fix. "Oh, my. Whatever happened to it?" I spoke quietly, since there was no need to upset the girl even more.

"It was my engagement ring." Tears sprang to her eyes anyway. "It got caught on the fabric. I only wanted to show my roommate. Next thing I knew . . ." She blinked, hoping to stave off the waterworks.

"There, there. It's okay. It's not your fault." Although technically it *was* her fault, she didn't need to hear that right now. "First things first. What's your name?"

"Amelia. Amelia Biggs."

"Well, here's what we're going to do, Amelia." I gently led her away from the counter, so she wouldn't have to face the ruined veil, and guided her to a sitting area in the middle of the shop. The space included a gilded coffee table between two armchairs slipcovered in white linen, and I gently deposited her in one chair, while I took the other. "I think I can fix it. When's your wedding?"

"That's the thing. It's Saturday . . . Saturday night." Sure enough, a fat tear rolled down the girl's cheek. "And I've made a mess of things. What am I going to do?"

I discreetly nudged a Kleenex box on the table toward her. "I'll tell you what we're *not* gonna do. We're not going to panic." Normally, the Kleenex came in handy for a much different reason, since mothers tended to burst into tears when they saw their daughter in a wedding veil for the first time.

"It happened last night. I thought I'd try everything on one more time, and I forgot to take off my ring." She yanked out a tissue.

"I see." I casually glanced down. An enormous diamond sparkled on the girl's left hand. It was a princess cut, about the size of a dime, and every bit as shiny. "You'd be surprised how many brides rip their veils. But it's usually at the reception, when someone dances on it."

She sniffled once or twice. Since she was growing calmer by the minute, I decided to keep up the chitchat. "I'll use fabric glue on the edges. The glue will bond the material back together again."

"But won't that show up under the lights?"

"Not at all. They make it with silicone now, which you can't see."

I searched my memory for any other tidbit to share, since my chitchat seemed to take her mind off her mistake. "You know, the Romans used glue on their clothes back in ancient days. You've seen those wreaths they wore? Those were bay laurel leaves dipped in gold. Then they stuck 'em together with an egg paste."

She'd stopped sniffling, so I must have been doing something right. "Really?"

"Yep. And then they gave 'em to their Olympic athletes. 'Course, the Greeks used glue too, but they made theirs with fish parts."

A tiny smile emerged at that. "You're kidding, right?"

"No, I'm not. I'm just thankful we've got synthetic adhesives now. Otherwise, I'd have to fix your veil with fish guts."

The smile spread. "And you promise no one will notice the rip?"

"Not a soul. Now, what's up with the rest of your wedding? Do you have everything else under control?"

"Well, to tell you the truth, it's been one thing after another. I had no idea it'd be this hard to plan a wedding."

Bless her heart. I could've told her it was like staging a military battle, and I wasn't even married yet. "Sounds like you've spent a whole year on it. That's a long time to wait for something."

"But it's not just the veil." She leaned closer, forgetting all about the tissue in her hand. "You won't believe what else has gone wrong. Hell's bells. Just last weekend, my piano player up and quit on me. She cut her hand. Can you believe it?"

"You don't say." My mind swirled at the coincidence. "You don't mean Prudence Fortenberry, do you?"

Her eyes widened. "Yeah. How'd you know it was her?"

"Simple. Only a few folks play at all the weddings around here. Did she tell you what happened to her hand?" Now that we'd staved off the waterworks, there was no harm in gleaning some information. Try as I might, I never could get Prudence to tell me how she injured herself.

"She said she cut it on a sharp piece of wood. She sounded pretty shook up."

"I can imagine. But did she say what she was doing when it happened?" While I didn't mean to pry—well, maybe I did—I'd wondered why Prudence wasn't more careful, since those fingers were her livelihood.

"No, she didn't tell me that part. I got the feeling it had to do with sports, though, because she said something about settling a score. To be honest . . . I kinda didn't care. I stopped listening when she said she couldn't play at my wedding."

"I understand. So, what did you do? Did you get someone else to play for you?"

"Hallelujah, yes. I found a guy in New Orleans. He's plays in a jazz band, but he can do classical too. He's charging me a thousand dollars. Can you believe it? 'Course, I didn't have much choice."

"Well, I'm sure it's all going to work out. I'll fix your veil this afternoon, and then I'll give you a call." I rose from the chair and padded over to the counter, where I plucked up the receipt I'd used during my telephone call with Beatrice. Once I returned, paper in hand, I passed it to her, along with a Bic. "Here. I just need your cell number. And try not to worry about anything else. Somehow, these things have a way of working out."

She dashed off a number, and then passed it to me as she rose. "Thank you so much. I don't know what I would've done if you weren't here today."

"No problem. Can you do me a favor, though? If anyone compliments your veil, can you please tell them you got it at my studio? I could use some of the good publicity with everything that's been going on around here."

Chapter 18

Once Amelia Biggs disappeared around the plywood opening—a whole lot happier than when she first arrived—I brought her veil and a big bottle of Fabri-Tac with me back to Ambrose's place.

Gluing the girl's veil back together would be simple enough, once I matched the edges up. Since fixing such a large a tear normally took the steady hands of a surgeon, not to mention the patience of a saint—neither of which I possessed—I decided to cheat and use Ambrose's standing press, which he kept in a corner of his studio. The machine would hold the pieces together while the glue dried, especially if I disabled the steam function by pulling the plug from the wall.

I crossed the room and rolled back the heavy lid. My fingers worked the tatters together bit by bit, and, after a while, Ambrose returned to the studio through the front door.

"Hey, there." He swung a white paper sack in his hand as he crossed the room.

I palmed the lace to hold the edges in place. "Whatcha got there?"

"Leftovers. Want one?"

I shook my head, since the last thing I needed was a reminder of his visit to Grady's doughnut shop. "No thanks. What did Lance say about my phone?"

"There's good news and bad news. Turns out whoever sent you that text used an outside website to deliver it. Which means the cops can trace it on the back end."

"That's good. So, what's the bad news?"

"It'll take some time and he needs to keep your phone this afternoon."

I frowned. "For how long?"

"He'll be done with it tonight. You can pick it up around six."
Ouch. "But I can't make it then. I promised Grady I'd meet up with him tonight, remember?"

Apparently, Ambrose hadn't remembered, because his face darkened. "Yeah. About that. You're still going to dinner with him?"

"I kinda promised him I would." I pretended to study the lace, so I wouldn't have to look at him.

"I see. I thought you would've changed your mind by now." His tone was icy.

"Look, Ambrose, there's no use for us to beat around the bush. You never said I couldn't date anyone else."

"But you didn't tell me until yesterday."

"I didn't even *know* until yesterday." It was a wonder I didn't burn another hole in the fabric with my staring, but I couldn't eye him just yet.

"So you're gonna go through with it?"

"I told you...I already said I would. Is there some reason I shouldn't?" Finally, I glanced up.

His jaw was tense, along with every other muscle in his neck and shoulders. It was typical Ambrose: He'd say one thing, while his whole body screamed something else.

"If you want me to call him and cancel, I will. But you'd better give me a darn good reason."

His jaw twitched ever so tightly, as he clenched it even tighter. It'd serve him right if he couldn't speak at all now.

"Well, if that's the case, maybe you *should* go," he finally said. "Have fun. Make a night of it. Hope you two have a great time. A fantastic time." He abruptly turned, his shoulders taut as a drum.

"Please don't be like that." I wanted to reach for him, but my ego got in the way. What if he shrugged away from me? Or, worse yet, ignored the gesture...as if my feelings didn't matter? "It's no big deal. Seriously. It's just a dinner between friends."

"I said I don't care. Just don't forget to lock the front door when you get home." He jerked around the table, but he wasn't paying attention, and his hip slammed into the left corner. He flinched, but it didn't stop him from walking away.

He didn't speak to me for the rest of the afternoon. I spent the hours holed up in the back half of the studio, where the fabric press, industrial sewing machine, and drafting table kept me company, while he commandeered the front half, with its cash register, pattern books, and client folders.

Finally, the clock showed it was ten minutes until five. *Close enough.* "Guess I'll be going." I brushed some eraser shavings from the sketch pad I'd been working on and rose.

Ambrose stood behind the counter, of course, speaking into his cell phone. Part of me wondered whether he was faking the conversation, though, because he gestured while he spoke, and he never did that otherwise. No doubt he only pretended to hold the conversation so he wouldn't have to speak with me. *The big phony.*

"I guess I'll see you later." I used a stage whisper as I crossed the room, doing my best to play along with him.

"Hm, mmm." He didn't even bother to glance up.

I mulled over his playacting—and everything else—on my drive back to the rent house. Why didn't he stop me from going out on my date tonight? Was it pride? Maybe. Stubbornness? Probably. Or, maybe he thought I needed to work something out of my system.

Whatever the reason, he was the world's worst liar. He could claim he didn't care all day long, but his wired jaw told me otherwise.

Lost in thought, I almost missed the driveway that led to our rent house and wrenched the steering wheel at the last possible moment. Normally, everything about our cottage cheered me when I pulled up the drive at night: from the lush bee balm that arced over the garden gate to the Emperor butterflies that played tag around it. Even the Pepto-Bismol–pink walls lifted my spirits, although the color seemed better suited to a Mexican hacienda than a shingled cottage in southern Louisiana.

Maybe it was the time of year, or, more likely, my foul mood, but tonight everything looked stark and gray as I parked and made my way up the walk. Bare vines straggled across the trellis and tapered out to withered points; the butterflies were gone, no doubt hiding in a nearby hackberry tree, and dusk muddied the home's pink walls to beige.

I slumped over the welcome mat and opened the door. By all rights, I should've dashed to the bathroom and spent some quality time with my makeup kit, since Grady would arrive in only a few minutes, but tonight my heart wasn't in it.

Maybe a snack will help. As I wandered through the living room on my way to the kitchen, I passed through a ghostly blue light that flickered over the walls. Ambrose must've come home at some point during the day and switched on the TV, only to forget about it on his way out the door. *How hypocritical.* Here he gave me a hard time for leaving the kitchen lights on the night before, when he couldn't be bothered to shut off a television set that ended up playing to an empty house all afternoon.

I reached for the remote, but a woman's voice stopped me cold.

". . . standing in the parking lot of a local shopping center."

Why, I'd know that voice anywhere. I slowly sank to the couch, the remote all but forgotten. Stormie Lanai appeared on the screen above me, resplendent with her fuchsia lipstick and fluttering eyelashes.

Over her shoulder lay the glass prism at the Factory, the clouds reflected in its shiny panes.

"Police found the murder weapon nearby." She gripped the mic tightly, doing her best to sound official. She even furrowed her brow for good measure. "According to a high-ranking detective, it belonged to a local shopkeeper by the name of Melissa DuBois."

A beat passed between my first and last names as she let the information sink in. She seemed proud to deliver the news, as if she were the one to break the story, when it was all over the *Bleu Bayou Impartial Reporter* the day before.

"Is the shopkeeper a suspect?" the disembodied voice of a male news anchor rang out.

She didn't respond right away. Instead, she frowned and pushed in her earpiece, as if she couldn't hear him. The question lingered in the air, hanging in the balance.

"Of course I'm not a suspect!" I yelled to the empty room. Although no one could hear me, especially not Stormie, I needed to defend myself.

"She's not at this time," Stormie finally said. Her eyes widened, as if she couldn't believe the news, either. "The police don't have a suspect, so the person is still at large. We need to take extra care over the next few days, folks. Don't forget we have a murderer on the loose."

She played the moment for all it was worth, but I couldn't even roll my eyes. She'd just linked my name to a murder, announcing to the world, or at least the good folks of Riversbend County, that I was the closest thing the police had to a suspect at this point.

Oh, shine. If a bride didn't doubt me before—and plenty did, judging by the number of canceled appointments—she would now. While Stormie claimed I wasn't a suspect, her body language said otherwise. I silently willed her to take it all back, to insist I was never under suspicion, but she didn't, which only encouraged viewers to jump to their own conclusions, no matter how misguided or uninformed.

I clicked off the remote and threw it to the ground. Of all the bad things to happen to me today, this had to be the worst. Even lower than finding my front door smashed in, or getting a text that crowed about the crime or bearing Ambrose's cold shoulder all afternoon.

Head lowered, I shuffled into the hall, aiming for the bedroom. If my motivation to dress for the dinner date with Grady was weak before, now it was nonexistent. I paused in front of my closet only long enough to grab the first thing I saw: a pair of gray wool slacks, navy silk blouse, and blue matching cardigan.

I threw on the clothes, remembering at the last moment how Grady mentioned my red sweater, but it puddled on the ground in a dirty heap, along with my blue jeans and a stained T-shirt. He'd have to be satisfied with the navy blouse and cardigan.

Once dressed, I meandered to the bathroom, where I dashed on some blush and added eyeliner. I was just about to reach for a tube of Chanel Rouge lipstick, when a knock sounded at the front door.

"Coming!" I slapped off the light and pasted a big, cheesy grin on my face. No doubt I looked like Tour Guide Barbie as I threw open the front door, but at this point I didn't care.

My mistake. Grady looked amazing. He wore a crisp periwinkle button-down, untucked, and a pair of tight True Religion blue jeans. Thick curls swept away from his face, finally free of the ever-present do-rag, and the porchlight cast gold highlights on the strands. Best of all, the smell of Armani's Acqua di Gio cologne reached me. The jeans, hair, and cologne were perfect, and I couldn't help but stare.

"Uh, hi.'"

Unlike me, Grady seemed perfectly at ease. "Hey, there."

"You look wonderful!"

"Isn't that supposed to be my line?" He bowed stiffly. "Missy, you look wonderful." He did a double-take when he noticed what I was wearing. "Thought you were going to give the red sweater a try."

"I was, but it needs to be dry-cleaned. Hope this is okay."

"Not a problem . . . you look great. Are you ready to go?"

Why didn't I spend more time getting ready? "Yeah. I think so. But would you like to come in first? I have some cold PBRs in the fridge."

"That sounds great, but I wanted to get us to the restaurant by six-thirty. There's something I want you to see."

"See?" I scrunched my nose. "Okay, then. Let me grab my purse."

I took my time sashaying to the kitchen, hoping he wouldn't notice the spring in my step, and grabbed a navy clutch from the counter. The purse felt lighter than air without a cell phone inside. "All set."

Once I locked the front door, we both headed for the driveway, where his sports car waited. The shiny Ford Mustang hovered over the pea gravel like a red balloon. Streamlined vents dimpled the hood and sensuous grooves ran up and over the wheel wells. The first time Beatrice spied the fastback at the doughnut store, she'd called it "sex on wheels" . . . and she was right.

Grady held open the passenger door while I entered the car, doing my best to keep my distance, when I wanted to bury my nose in his neck and inhale for all I was worth.

Once on Highway 18, we drove east, toward downtown. The large pin oaks alongside the freeway blotted out what was left of the afternoon sun. After a few awkward moments, when the only sound in the cab was the downshifting of gears, we began to chat about work, Bleu Bayou and, of course, the murder investigation.

"So, what's going on with it?" Grady shot me a glance as he drove.

"Lance's doing his best, but he doesn't have any suspects yet. He brought in Bettina Leblanc last night as a person of interest, but only because she had a big fight with Charlotte on New Year's Eve. He told me he wanted to re-create the murder scene today over at the parking lot."

"I was thinking about that." Grady maneuvered the car around a curve while he spoke, and soon the old Sweetwater mansion appeared up ahead. Dusk faded the grand columns until they melded into the house behind them. "Seems to me you'd have to be pretty strong to get a body into a whiskey barrel like that."

"You know . . . you're right. Then, again, maybe the person had help."

We both considered that as the car roared past Sweetwater and then approached Dippin' Donuts. Like the mansion, the shop looked asleep, with dark windows and empty walkways. The only light came from a neon arrow that shot from the shop's roof.

"Come to think of it . . . someone probably did help the murderer." I scrunched my nose again. "Even if I thought Bettina did it—which I don't—she'd have a hard time lifting a body all by herself. And, Lance told me there weren't any drag marks on the ground. I can't imagine any of the ladies Charlotte worked with being strong enough to maneuver a body like that."

Then again, a big guy like Paxton Haney could lift Charlotte on his own. It was something to think about as we drove past Dippin' Donuts and then zoomed past the Factory, the last vestiges of downtown disappearing in the side-view mirror.

"By the way . . . where're we going?" I finally asked.

"You'll see. Patience, young grasshopper."

I thought about swatting his arm, but didn't. While I could swat and poke and pinch Ambrose to my heart's content, I didn't know Grady well enough. Not yet, anyway.

Instead, I gazed at the landscape, which morphed from city to country with the arrival of sugarcane fields. Leftover stalks—remnants from the recent harvest—littered the ground around us like brown matchsticks drizzled from a giant box of Diamond wooden strikes.

After a few more miles, the fields gave way to a petroleum plant. Here, shiny metal tubes crisscrossed overhead, glinting in the dusk like a jungle gym on an empty playground. Even though the plant was built in the 1950s, the facility looked abandoned, skeletal; as if no one ever completed it. On its far end sat a smokestack, the fire on its top no doubt started by those imaginary matches I'd pictured in the sugarcane fields.

Finally, Grady made a hard right and we pulled off the road.

My eyes widened when I spotted a sign for Antoine's Country Kitchen. "Shut my mouth and call my Shirley!" Subtlety was *not* my strong suit.

Chapter 19

While Antoine's Country Kitchen looked like a fish-camp bunkhouse—complete with corrugated tin roof, wraparound porch, and walls hewn from unvarnished planks—it was known far and wide for its food, not its ambience. Even the Food Network crowned it the best Cajun seafood in the South, which was like naming one small kitchen in Italy the best pizza place of all.

"It gets better." Grady spoke in a rush, as he switched off the engine and hopped from the car. "C'mon." He quickly moved to the passenger side, where he opened the door for me and whisked me to my feet. "Let's go."

We practically ran across the asphalt. When we reached the front porch, the hardwoods underneath vibrated from music that poured through gaps in the plain wood walls. It was the wheezy strains of an accordion, accompanied by the clack of a metal spoon hitting a rubboard.

"They have live music on Wednesdays. It's zydeco night." Grady's eyes were shining.

He pulled me along as he made his way through the entrance, which fanned open to reveal a large dining room and dance hall. To our left sat a recessed stage, complete with wood-paneled walls, indoor-outdoor carpet, and a large Louisiana state flag stapled to the ceiling. Higher still was exposed ductwork that snaked in and out of the rafters, while below our feet lay acid-washed concrete.

It felt like a warehouse, only countrified, with picnic tables for seating and posters of famous zydeco bands, like Buckwheat Zydeco, Dr. John, and Boozoo Chavis on the walls. I even spied a limp fishing net on one wall that was stuffed with fake blue crabs.

Talk about kitschy. "This place sure is something," I said vaguely.

Grady chuckled as he led me to a picnic table by the stage. Apparently the Cajun Country Stomp Swampers—so named by a plastic banner that hung behind the band's heads—featured an accordion, rubboard, fiddle, and singer. I didn't see a guitar player until we sat down, since an old man with a rubboard blocked him from my view.

"Jambalaya, des tartes d'ecreuvisse," crooned the singer. He wore a red vest and flared blue jeans and his baritone was thick and murky, like a bowl of Cajun gumbo. *"Par a soir moi . . ."*

Grady waited for the song to finish, and then he began to translate for me. " 'Jambalaya and a crawfish pie, 'cause tonight I'm gonna see my sweetest one. Pick guitar, fill fruit jar . . . son of a gun, we'll have big fun on the bayou.' It doesn't get much more Cajun than that, does it?" He laughed. "That's why I love this place so much. By the way, I can't believe you've never been here."

"I don't get out much." I stared straight ahead, overly conscious of his gaze.

"That can't be true. I'll bet you head over to New Orleans and Baton Rouge all the time."

"Not when everything I want is right in Bleu Bayou." I quickly swallowed. *Where did that come from?*

"I know what you mean," he said. "I went to high school there. Never really left, to tell you the truth."

"Jouer l'guitar . . ." Apparently the singer had moved beyond the chorus, and he practically kissed the microphone when he launched into another verse.

"Um . . . I don't see any menus." Hopefully, my feeble attempt at conversation sounded more natural than it felt. *How can I concentrate with Grady's face so close to mine?* "What do you think I should order?"

He finally leaned back and pointed to a chalkboard under the picture of Buckwheat Zydeco. "The menu's right there. I've only been here once. The shrimp étouffée's pretty good, if you like your food spicy. 'Course, there's always the fried frog legs."

I playfully swatted his arm. *To heck with formalities.* "Don't you dare!"

"Well, now. I'll just have to order it."

Funny . . . I never noticed the way his eyes twinkled when he smiled. Or that his teeth were perfectly straight and beautifully white.

I pretended to listen as he read aloud from the menu. He was definitely good-looking. Maybe not my type, since my type called to mind words like *tall, dark, and handsome*, but he had the blond, fair, and rugged thing down pat. And, although good looks weren't the most important thing, it wouldn't hurt to have such a nice view with dinner.

As soon as he rose to place our order—two plates of shrimp étoufée with homemade potato salad—I tore my eyes away and finally glanced around the room.

By now, several couples had abandoned their picnic tables for the dance floor. The men took hold of their partners' waists and began to shuffle them back and forth, with an occasional twirl thrown in. Unlike other two-steps I'd seen, like the Texas two-step, this version required people to move in a tight square, always an arm's-length apart.

After a while, my gaze moved past the dancers to the rubboard player behind them. The old man sat on a folding chair and the instrument covered his chest like a tin breastplate. He'd braided his nubby gray hair into dreadlocks that dipped and swayed as he strummed a spoon across the board's ridges. At the same time, he thumped the surface with the knuckles of his left hand . . . so enthusiastically, I worried he'd scrape the skin right off his fingers.

Clack, shuffle, scrape. Scrape, shuffle, clack. It sounded like a tap dancer on hardwoods. By the end of the song, he was still swaying, even though the singer had switched from Hank Williams to "My Girl Josephine," and that's when Grady reappeared at our table.

"What's so funny?" He held a laminated number, which he stuck in a metal holder attached to the table's side.

"Nothing . . . I'm just enjoying the band." Truth be told, zydeco sounded an awful lot like an Irish jig. "What took you so long?"

"I ran into an old friend from high school." He pointed to the counter, where a balding man in a letterman's jacket chatted with a waitress. "Believe it or not, that guy used to play receiver when I quarterbacked."

The man's jacket—made of crackled white leather with faded orange felt sleeves—strained to close over his ample stomach.

Grady scowled. "He was the reason we lost at State."

"You don't say." Compared to his classmate, Grady looked ten years younger. He didn't have an ounce of fat on him—at least that I could see—not to mention those beautiful, thick curls.

I flinched. *Shame on me for being so shallow.* I didn't know the stranger in the letterman's jacket from Adam, and I had no right to compare him to Grady like that.

"Missy?"

"What? I'm sorry. I wasn't paying attention. You were saying?"

"I went to high school with that guy. Kinda a loser."

My smile faded a bit. "Why would you say that?"

"He never should've dropped that pass for the title. It was a rocket. Straight down the middle. I still get on him about it sometimes."

"Wow. You have an amazing memory." I quickly calculated the number of years between that pass and tonight's dinner. At least fifteen had come and gone since then. "Uh, Grady? When did you graduate from high school?"

"A while ago. Probably the same year as you."

I knew it. He was in his thirties too. Which was a little old to be reminiscing about a high school football game. "Seems to me you'd let bygones be bygones after so many years."

"Yeah, but he's still a loser. I mean . . . look at him. He dresses like a slob."

Just then, Grady's classmate said something funny to the waitress behind the counter, and she threw back her head to laugh.

"He seems like a nice enough guy," I said. "At least the waitress thinks so."

"Enough about him. Speaking of clothes . . . you really should wear that red sweater more often. It looks great with your hair. Maybe I could take you shopping sometime."

I was about to demur when a waitress appeared at our table with enormous plates of shrimp étouffée She balanced the heavy dishes effortlessly, using only her wrists.

"Étouffée?"

"Yes, please."

She slid my plate down her fingers and onto the table in one smooth motion.

"Now, that's impressive," I said.

She grinned, and then she did the same thing with Grady's plate. "Can I get you two anything else?"

"No, I think we're fine." Although the smell of jalapeño wafted up from the plate, it didn't make my nose itch, like the dish had at Hank Dupre's party.

Grady nodded his thanks to the waitress. "Smells good. Let's dig in."

The minute we began to eat, Grady launched into a running commentary about the dancers around us. The first time he criticized a pair, I started to interject, but he wouldn't let me get a word in edgewise. The next time it happened, I gave up and nibbled on a shrimp instead. Funny, but the food didn't seem nearly as appealing now, and the longer he talked, the less I ate.

According to Grady, almost every dancer on the floor had two left feet and didn't deserve to be seen dancing in public. His remedy was a beginner's dance class, like the one he'd taken at Bleu Bayou Community College. Apparently, *he* was an excellent dancer.

Once he finally stopped talking, he shoved his plate aside and rose. "C'mon, let's go show 'em how it's done."

Although it *would* provide a break from the running monologue, it might also encourage him, which I no longer wanted to do. "No, I didn't think that's a good idea." We obviously had very different ideas about how this date should go.

"It'll be fun." He grabbed my hand and pulled me to my feet before I could protest.

Before I knew it, we were twirling around the dance floor like tumbleweeds, spinning from one end to the next, the room a blur of colors and sounds. Unlike everyone else, we traveled from one corner of the dance hall to the other, which soon made me light-headed.

"Whoa." I stopped mid-twirl and held up my hand. "I need to sit down."

"C'mon. You're fine. We're just getting started." He tried to pull me close again, but I held my ground.

"No, really. I need to sit down." I pivoted and began to walk back to the table, not knowing, or caring, whether he would follow me.

I plopped on the bench and laid my head on my hands. Little did I know when Grady picked me up at the house, I'd be desperate to get back after only a few hours. Because, right now, I wanted nothing more than to go home. Home to Ambrose. Home to someone who'd actually listen to me and who actually cared about what I had to say. Someone who would think about more than what I looked like, or what I wore.

"What's wrong with you?" He sounded angry.

"Nothing's wrong with me. Can you please take me home?"

"You just got a little dizzy. I can move pretty fast."

"No, I don't think that's it." I finally looked at him and spied a clock over his shoulder, which was shaped like a giant Budweiser bottle cap. Hallelujah, the night was still young.

"But I don't want to go yet." His tone had turned whiny. "I thought we'd dance a little, maybe have a few drinks. You know, get to know each other."

"You're kidding, right? You haven't asked a single question about me or my life all night."

"That's not true. I asked you what you wanted to eat. That's a question."

Oh, brother. "Look, I don't feel well. Please take me home."

"Fine. If that's how you want it." He turned and began to stalk across the room, barreling between several couples on the dance floor.

I lost sight of him for a while, but he reappeared when the song ended and the dancers began to disperse. He stood by the exit, so I skirted around the edges of the room until I reached him and even threw him a tight-lipped smile for good measure. Judgmental or not, Grady was my ride home, which meant I had to be civil for at least ten more minutes.

The moment I caught up with him, he shoved past another couple who'd walked into the restaurant. His elbow smacked the woman's shoulder, which caused her to wobble on her stiletto heels, but he didn't even bother to apologize.

"I'm so sorry." I turned to look at the woman's date, who'd wrapped his arm around her waist protectively. "Mr. Haney? Is that you?"

"Why, hello." He looked surprised to see me too. "Didn't expect to see you here tonight."

"I guess not."

The moment his date realized what was happening, she inched behind Paxton's back, hoping to hide behind his bulky sport coat. She also ducked her head, although I'd recognize that pixie haircut anywhere.

"Brooke? What're you doing here?"

The photographer reluctantly stepped out from behind his shoulder. "Hi, Missy."

Why in the world is Brooke Champagne, the photographer who owns Brooke's Bridal Portraits, going out to dinner with Paxton Haney? While she normally wore cargo pants and Birkenstocks at her studio, tonight she'd opted for a black leather miniskirt and spiky heels.

The music dimmed around me as I struggled to make sense of it all.

"Um . . . we're meeting about a client." Paxton spoke slowly, clearly improvising. "That's it. We're having a business dinner about a client."

"Really? Which one?" I asked.

They both answered me at the same time.

"The Fitzgeralds," he said.

"A chamber gala." Brooke immediately slapped her hand over her mouth.

Paxton quickly interjected. "You see . . . uh . . . the Fitzgeralds are helping to put on a chamber gala, and they asked us both to work on the project. That's it."

I had to hand it to him; he was quick with an excuse. "I see. Well, I was just on my way out. So nice to see you two again." I quickly moved away from them, my mind reeling.

Of course, Paxton Haney had every right to ask Brooke out on a date; he was a grown man, after all. But it seemed so soon after Charlotte's death, especially since he had to plan a funeral *and* work on the sale of his business with Hank Dupre.

And they were hiding something. That much was clear. But what?

The sooner I got back to the cottage and called Lance to discuss it, the better I'd feel about it.

Chapter 20

After enduring a ten-minute car ride with Grady, during which time he didn't speak to me, I finally arrived at the rent house. I barely had time to close the passenger door before he roared off again in a cloud of pea-gravel dust and engine exhaust.

Thankfully, a light blazed in our living room window, which meant Ambrose was home. Just thinking about him spurred my steps, and I hurried through the door and into the cottage, where I found him standing by the kitchen counter.

He held his favorite Auburn University coffee mug waist-high. "What're you doing home already?"

"I'm so glad you're here!" I didn't even bother to pretend everything was fine. Instead, I flung my purse on the counter and rushed to his side.

"Whoa. Rough night?"

"You wouldn't believe it if I told you." I wrapped my arms around his waist and hugged him tightly, even with the coffee cup in his hand.

"What was that for?" He looked confused, although a smile played on his lips.

"For being you. Here. Gimme that." I motioned for the mug, which he gladly handed over. "This has been one of the longest nights of my life, and it's only seven-thirty."

"You don't say. So, Grady wasn't a fun date?"

"Not even close." I took a sip. Although lukewarm, the coffee was the best thing I'd tasted all night. Even Antoine's famous fare couldn't make up for Grady's nonstop chatter. "I thought he'd be fun to talk to. He seems so easygoing at the doughnut shop. Boy, was I wrong."

"Let me guess: He talked about himself the whole time."

"Bingo." I set the mug down. "How'd you know that, by the way?"

"It's not rocket science. Look at the guy. He must spend half his life at the gym and the other half at a tanning salon."

I playfully swatted his arm, which felt completely natural. "It wasn't just that. When he finally *did* stop talking about himself, it was only to criticize other people. Heavens to Betsy, that man has an opinion about everybody."

"Bet that got old *real* fast."

"You have no idea." I winced. "He even talked about a high school football game. High school! That was, what? Fifteen years ago?"

"Maybe those were his best days. Maybe he thought you'd be impressed."

"Well, he was wrong." I frowned when I remembered something else. "That's not all that happened. You'll never guess who I ran into at the restaurant. It was Brooke Champagne and Paxton Haney."

"Together?"

"Looked like it, and they were definitely on a date. You should've seen Brooke's skirt."

"Doesn't she wear baggy pants and those hippie sandals when she photographs people?"

"She does. Only tonight, she was dressed in a leather miniskirt and some snazzy Manalo Blahniks. And do you wanna know what I find really weird? Brooke should be angry with Paxton, since his cousin wanted to add a photography studio to their business. That would give people like Brooke more competition. But, no. Instead of being mad at him, she goes out to dinner with him. All chummy, like it wasn't their first time."

"That *is* weird." Ambrose thought it over before pointing to something on the counter. "By the way, I got your phone back. I knew you'd want to catch up on your texts when you got home."

"Ambrose." I moved to hug him again. "That was so sweet of you. And after everything that happened this afternoon . . ."

"Don't mention it. I think we should forget all about what happened tonight. What's done is done. Seems like you survived your date, even if your ears got a real workout."

"Deal. By the way . . . I'm starving. I lost my appetite when he started talking, so I didn't eat much. He even took me to that Cajun restaurant way out past the power plant."

"Antoine's? What a waste. They're supposed to have great food."

"What little I ate was pretty tasty. Wanna get some dinner with me?"

"You bet." He reached into the pocket of his jeans for his car keys. He wore the same brand as Grady, only his weren't nearly as tight, or as perfectly pressed. "You don't have to ask me twice. What're you in the mood for?"

"I want to go someplace familiar. No more surprises tonight."

"Let's hit up Odilia's, then. We both know the menu, and she'll be glad to see you if she's working tonight."

I smiled at him gratefully. "Perfect."

He'd managed to cheer me up in two minutes flat.

Why did I think someone like Grady could offer me anything better?

Chapter 21

We pulled into the parking lot of Miss Odilia's Southern Eatery not long afterward. Almost every space was taken, even on a Wednesday night, so Ambrose parked his Audi near the back and then walked to the passenger side to whoosh open the car door for me.

Unlike Antoine's rustic warehouse style, Odilia's restaurant was homey and warm. Once we made it through the parking lot, we passed purple flower boxes bursting with trumpet-like foxglove and full-bodied caladiums and then walked under a scalloped awning that ruffled and swayed in the breeze.

We stepped through the entrance and into the foyer, where we spied Odilia behind a hostess stand crafted from an old church podium. The stand's wood matched the finish on a Baldwin piano positioned next to it, flush with the wall.

Tonight, Odilia wore an elegant cobalt pantsuit instead of her normal chef's coat, and she grinned the moment she saw us. "Look what the cat dragged in!"

"Hi, Odilia."

"Come here so I can greet you properly." She scooted out from behind the stand and enveloped me in a warm hug. The smell of Aqua Net hairspray reached me, and her dangly earrings brushed against my cheek.

"It's so good to see you, Odilia." When she finally released me, I glanced at Ambrose.

"Look who I brought."

"It's Mr. Jackson," she said. "My, oh my. This is a special night."

"Evenin', Miss Odilia." Ambrose held out his hand, since they didn't know each other well enough for a hug. While I'd known Odilia since childhood, the two of them only met six months ago.

"What brings you two here tonight?" she asked.

"Isn't there only one right answer? For the good cookin', of course." Every time I ate at her place, Odilia asked me the same question, and every time I gave her the same answer. We never tired of the banter, although I couldn't speak for Ambrose.

"Come on then," she said. "Let's get you seated and get some dinner in you."

She led us through the dining room, past couples, families, and even singles, to an empty table about halfway back. Before I caught up with her, I felt a hand on my shoulder.

"Missy!"

I turned to see Bettina Leblanc. Like always, she'd wound her hair into a tight ballerina bun and she wore no-nonsense blue jeans. Other than that, though, she seemed transformed. Relaxed. It was the first time I'd seen her smile in days.

"What're you doing here?" I asked. Although the answer was obvious, since she stood in front of a table littered with plates and silverware, I didn't expect to see her at Odilia's restaurant so soon. Not after her fight with Charlotte, which landed her smack-dab at the top of a suspect list in the murder investigation.

"Celebrating." She gestured to her table, where an older man sat. He wore stylish, unframed glasses, and he seemed vaguely familiar. "Have you met my accountant? Missy, this is Sheridan."

Aha. "Nice to meet you." I'd noticed him around the Factory, since he usually carried a bulky briefcase that looked ready to explode at any moment. Normally, we passed each other in the parking lot. "I thought you looked familiar."

"You too," he answered. "You own the hat studio, right?"

"Yep. I'm downstairs from Bettina, on the other side of the building."

"Who does your books?"

I grinned at his chutzpah. "I've had the same accountant for a few years now. I'll let you know if anything changes with that, though."

"Speaking of books . . ." Bettina's voice was light and breezy. "We were going over mine. Now that I've been cleared by the police, I can finally get back to business. What a relief."

I cocked my head. "Cleared? What happened?" As far as I knew, Lance still considered Bettina a person of interest. She was one of the last people to see Charlotte alive, and their meeting was anything but friendly.

"Want to join us and I'll tell you all about it?"

I glanced over to Ambrose, who stood with Odilia by an empty table. While I wanted more than anything to find out the reason for Bettina's sudden transformation, I also needed some downtime with him to bring us back to an even keel.

"I'd love to, but I promised Ambrose I'd have dinner with him tonight."

"Then I'll give you the short version," she said. "They finally got subpoenas for the video from the parking lot and my computer records."

"We have a video camera in our parking lot?" *First things first.* I'd never noticed one, although they could've hidden a camera in one of the fake gas lamps that dotted the lot.

She nodded. "Uh-uh. But only in the main lot, not the employee one. Which is too bad, since the police could've used one there." She sighed happily. "None of that matters anymore, though. Once they got a subpoena for the film, they analyzed the time stamp. It shows I didn't get to work until after ten on New Year's Day. I kinda had a few drinks the night before."

Realization dawned. *Of course.* According to Odilia, Bettina definitely was drunk on New Year's Eve. No doubt she nursed a nasty hangover the next morning, when Charlotte was murdered. "That's great, Bettina! So the police know exactly when you came to the Factory. But . . ."

"I know what you're thinking." She shot me a look I couldn't quite read. "Just to be sure, they got hold of my computer records. I must've been ordering some supplies, because I was definitely online for most of the morning."

"Those things seem so obvious. Why didn't they check them before?"

She shrugged. "Well, it takes some time to get subpoenas down here, for one thing. And Detective LaPorte spent most of his time worrying about the back lot, since that's where the murder happened. He even re-created the murder scene, if I'm not mistaken. I don't blame him for what he did. I'm just glad it got sorted out."

"Well, I do." Sheridan spoke over the top of his champagne glass, which he'd raised to his lips. "I told her she should sue the police department. They put her through two days of hell . . . and for what? In the meantime, they could've been focusing on the real killer." He threw back his head and polished off his glass in a single gulp.

"Now, Sheridan." Bettina's rebuff was gentle. "No one's suing anyone. I'm just glad they finally came around. I was worried I might have to sell the bakery. The gossips around here would've shut me down for sure."

"But it didn't come to that." Sheridan returned his empty flute to the table. "We'll accrue for your losses over the next few weeks. Shouldn't take much longer than that to catch up."

"I'm so happy for you, Bettina." While I wanted to stay and hear even more about her newfound joy, I couldn't keep Ambrose waiting forever. Knowing him, he hadn't had much to eat today, either. "We'll have to have coffee soon and catch up. Nice to finally meet you . . . uh, Sheridan."

Bettina left me no choice but to call him by his first name. Hopefully, he wouldn't tease me, like Hank Dupre always did.

"Nice to meet you too. Let me know if you ever need any help. Bettina has my number."

I left the two of them behind as I made my way to Ambrose and Odilia. Once more, the day had taken such a strange and unexpected turn.

"What's wrong?" Ambrose asked, once I caught up to them.

"Nothing. It's actually good news. Bettina isn't a suspect anymore in Charlotte's murder."

"But what about the fight?" Odilia's eyes narrowed. "I'm telling you, those two were going at it like cats and dogs. Thought I was going to have to get in-between 'em and break it up."

"But that's the thing, Odilia." My gaze traveled to her. "Bettina was home nursing a hangover the next morning. Lance finally got the videotape from the parking lot and it shows she didn't show up to work until after ten."

Ambrose blanched. "That sounds good on the face of it. But who's to say she didn't enter the building and then go out back afterward?" He threw up his hands. "Not that I think she had anything to do with it. I like her as much as you do."

"Don't worry. I wondered the same thing." I took the chair Odilia had pulled away from the table. "Guess Lance also got her computer records from the Internet provider. Her IP address shows she was on-line when Charlotte was murdered. It took a while for the files to come in, but they finally did."

"Glad to hear it," Odilia said. "Just wish they'd catch the person once and for all. Makes me jittery knowing we have a murderer out there."

"Trust me, Odilia. Your son's working on it. It doesn't quite work like it does on TV. He can't solve a crime in thirty minutes or less, and then they roll the credits."

Odilia chuckled. "As long as we don't have to stay tuned 'til next week, I'll be happy. So, here y'all go. I'll have Cherise wait on you tonight. She's new here."

She waited while Ambrose pulled out his chair and settled into it. "By the way, I can't believe you're the one who found that body too, Missy. Seems like you have a knack for finding dead bodies."

I was about to protest, but Ambrose spoke first.

"She does, doesn't she? People are going to wonder if it happens again. They'll think she's the angel of death or something."

It took some serious restraint on my part not to swat him again. "I'm not that bad. And I can't help it if I keep getting lassoed into these situations. Maybe I'm like that boy in the movie . . . you know, the one who sees dead people."

"I hope not. Besides, we're here to take a break from all that talk about death. Tonight we're here to relax and enjoy a good meal." He turned to Odilia. "Missy here got stuck with a serial talker tonight. Figure she needs some downtime to recuperate."

"That's a shame," she said. "Should I bring a nice bottle of wine to take the edge off?"

"Definitely. A good Bordeaux, if you have it."

"Sure I shouldn't bring two bottles?"

"Nuh-uh." I jumped in, trying to keep those two from clouding what was left of my clear head. "It's tempting. But, no thank you. I still have to call your son when we're done here, and I don't want to slur my speech."

"I don't think he'd mind," she said. "You've seen each other in all kinds of situations. Some pretty, some not. That's what happens when you've been friends for so long."

I glanced at Ambrose. "You're right. If someone really likes you, nothing you do can change that. At least, nothing within limits."

"It's all part of the package." He placed his hand over mine. "The good, the bad, and . . . like you said . . . sometimes the ugly."

We eyed each other for several seconds, until Odilia chuckled. "Looks like you two need to get a room. You're getting all moony and you haven't even had your wine yet. Honestly, this is a family restaurant." She planted her hands on her hips, but her tone was teasing.

"No promises," Ambrose said.

"Then I'd better send over your server. Maybe she can chaperone you two."

Ambrose waited for Odilia to walk away before he squeezed my hand. "C'mere, you. We never did kiss and make up after our fight."

He leaned in to kiss me. I'm pretty sure it lasted only a nanosecond or two before we parted again, although I wanted it to last a whole lot longer. I didn't notice a waitress had approached our table until she delicately cleared her throat.

"Ahem. I'm Cherise, and I'll be your server tonight."

I suppressed a giggle. *Why does Ambrose always make me feel like a schoolgirl?* Every time he came close, a tickle automatically formed at the back of my throat and butterflies somersaulted through my stomach. Maybe it was his kiss, or perhaps the cologne he wore, which threw me off-kilter. He wore the same kind as Grady, only it smelled ten times better on him.

"Miss Odilia is bringing us a bottle of Bordeaux," he said. Unlike me, he recovered in a flash. "And we already know what we'd like to order. We'll both have the fried chicken and maybe a basket of her famous rolls to go with it."

The girl quickly scribbled a few notes and left.

"Now, where were we?" Ambrose turned around the minute she walked away.

"We were making up." I sighed heavily. "But, I have to excuse myself for a minute." While I wanted to stay put right here, seated only inches away from him, I couldn't ignore something else a moment longer. "I really hate to do this, but I've *got* to visit the ladies' room. I didn't have time when we were at our house, and Grady wouldn't stop talking long enough for me to get away earlier."

Reluctantly, I rose and stepped behind Ambrose's chair, my finger trailing along his shoulder blades. "Promise you won't touch the wine until I get back."

"For you, anything. Just don't take too long, or I might get lonely out here."

It took a few steps for the room to right itself again, given my light-headedness. I aimed for a hallway on the other side of the restaurant, which housed the restrooms and a storage closet. A few steps into the journey, I passed a table with an elderly couple who hung matching canes over the backs of their chairs. The next table held a family of four, including two children. The kids looked surprisingly clean, given the carpet under their table held bread crumbs, spilled milk, and a smashed roll or two.

I chuckled as I continued, one table away from my destination. A sharp voice rose above the hubbub before I could reach it, though.

"I tell you, that girl wasn't worth spit."

Chapter 22

I was so startled, I almost tripped. The speaker used the exact phrase as the texter who railed against Charlotte earlier on my cell phone.

"Well, she's gone." Now a man spoke, his voice quick and desperate. "You don't have to worry about her anymore. We took care of her. And no one saw us kill her."

Slowly, I turned. Trudi Whidbee sat at the last table before the hall, the expensive Russian sable casually slung behind her chair. Across from her sat Barrett, her fiancé, who looked about as miserable as the wet weather outside.

She jabbed her finger against his chest, which made him shrivel even more into his dress shirt. "Did you think I wouldn't find out about your little affair with Charlotte? How stupid do you think I am? At least you had the good sense to follow my plan. Now that she's dead, I'll never have to wonder about you two again."

She didn't notice me while she spoke, which was just as well, since I couldn't move my feet anyway.

"Aren't you gonna say something?" she spat.

His lips barely cleared the collar of his shirt by now. "I told you I was sorry. Really, really sorry. I've said it a million times. And I helped you kill her. What more do you want from me?"

"I want you to promise it'll never happen again. Honestly, I don't know what you ever saw in her. She wasn't worth spit. That much's for sure."

My breath stalled as I absorbed the words again. *Of course. It all makes sense now.*

Carefully, I lifted my right foot and slid it back an inch or two. Part of me wanted to run right back to Ambrose and blurt out what I'd heard, but another part wanted to hear more.

Barrett eyed Trudi's finger warily, as if it might bite him. "I made a mistake. A really bad mistake. But she's gone now. It's over. Why can't we go back to the way things were before?"

"Before?" She laughed, but it was brittle. "Before? We killed a woman, Barrett. We can't go back to the way things were 'before.'"

I'd heard enough. My breath still lodged in my throat, I brought my left foot back to meet the right. Inch by inch, I slid away from their table, careful to avoid any sudden moves.

When I finally reached the family with the messy carpet, I exhaled a ragged breath. After striding several more yards, I pulled up next to Ambrose.

He noticed something was wrong right away. "What's up? You look like you've seen Blackbeard's ghost."

"Worse than that." I fumbled for his shoulder again, only now it wasn't to caress his skin. Now I needed something to hold me up. "I just found out who killed Charlotte Devereaux."

"Come again?"

I pressed harder against his shoulder. "Trudi Whidbee is here. I heard her talking with her fiancé. She's one of the brides who hired Charlotte to plan her wedding. Only it sounds like her fiancé had an affair with Charlotte instead. So Trudi killed Charlotte. Not only that, but she made her fiancé help her do it."

"Whoa. Slow down. Have a seat." He pulled out my chair and patted the seat cushion. "You're as pale as a bedsheet."

I shook my head, even though he was right. "We don't have time. I need to call Lance. Now. Before they get away."

"Hold on a second." His eyes narrowed. "Sit down first and take some deep breaths. Otherwise, you're going to faint."

Reluctantly, I did as I was told. By now, I should've recognized the signs of shock: the shallow breath, the tunnel vision, the knot in my stomach that forced bile into my throat. I felt the same way when I discovered Charlotte's body in the whiskey barrel behind my studio only two days ago.

"Put your head between your knees," he ordered. "Now."

I followed his instructions to a T. After several deep breaths, the sound of blood whooshing through my ears softened.

"How's that? Do you feel better?"

I nodded, which wasn't easy, given my position. "I think so." By the time I straightened, I could finally breathe normally again. "Thank you. I needed that."

"Now, start from the beginning. What happened to you back there?"

"Okay. Here goes." I inhaled another breath for good measure. "Remember that text I got? The one from someone who bragged about getting rid of Charlotte? It said, 'CD wasn't worth spit.' Those exact words. I haven't heard that phrase in a million years. And it's what Trudi said back at her table just now."

"You don't think it's a coincidence?"

"No, I don't. They admitted to killing her. And he kept apologizing and saying they wouldn't have to worry about her anymore."

"Bottom line is, those two had an affair and the spurned bride took her revenge. With her fiancé's help. That's what you're telling me?"

"Exactly."

"Okay, let's say you're right. But what kind of man gets together with another woman right before his wedding?"

I shrugged. "Apparently, Barrett Hudson does."

Something else niggled at the back of my mind as I spoke: A memory that slipped in and out of my consciousness before I could catch it. Something about a telephone call I placed at the studio. A desperate call; one I didn't want to make.

Finally, the memory crystallized. It was a call to Trudi after she canceled her appointment. I tried to talk her out of it, but she turned the tables on me and accused *me* of introducing her and Barrett to Charlotte in the first place.

Even more images crystallized. The two of us sitting in Bettina's bakery the day before. Where she once more blamed me for bringing Charlotte into her life. While she managed to sound calm while we spoke, she gouged an inch-wide scratch in a photograph under her fingernail.

And then, a final memory surfaced: the beautiful French door at my studio, smashed into a million pieces that glittered on the welcome mat. "Lorda mercy!"

"What now?" Ambrose took my hand in his.

"Trudi's the one who destroyed my door. She blamed me for getting them involved with Charlotte. She thinks I'm part of the reason her fiancé cheated on her!"

He tightened his grip. "Okay, I've heard enough. You need to get on the phone right now. Call your friend Lance and tell him what you've told me." He lifted my purse from the ground with his free hand and fished out my cell. "Want me to dial for you?"

"No, I've got it." I reached for the phone, although my own hand was shaking. "He's on my speed dial."

I tapped the screen and waited through three rings before Lance picked up.

"Hi, Missy. What's up?" He sounded breezy, since he had no idea why I'd called.

"I know who killed Charlotte Devereaux, Lance." The words came out in a rush. "She's here at your mom's restaurant, with her fiancé."

He didn't respond right away.

"Lance? Did you hear me? I said I know who killed her."

"I know what you said." He paused again. "I'm just trying to wrap my head around it. Okay. Tell me what happened."

I proceeded to tell Lance everything I knew about Charlotte Devereaux and Barrett Hudson. About what Trudi Whidbee said and how she angry she'd been. When I finally came up for air, I was met by more silence. "Well, aren't you gonna say something?"

"Definitely. Stay right where you are. Don't move a muscle. I'll be there in five minutes."

"I know this all sounds crazy."

He didn't sound entirely convinced.

"But I really think they killed her, and they were the ones who destroyed the door to my studio. You can't miss her when you get to the restaurant. She's got this enormous fur coat . . . it's a black Russian sable."

"Got it. And promise me you won't try to approach them. Are you there by yourself?"

"No, Ambrose is with me. We came for dinner, and then I ran into Trudi when I went to use the ladies' room."

"Put him on the phone."

Silently, I passed the cell to Ambrose. He shot me a funny look but took it, nevertheless.

"Hello?"

"Of course," he said a few moments later. Then he eyed me, which only confirmed what I suspected about their conversation. "I'll do my best to keep her in check. Just get here quick."

Ambrose clicked off the line and handed me the phone. "He'll be here in a few. We're supposed to sit tight and let him handle it when he gets here."

"Did he tell you to keep me away from them?" I couldn't hide the irritation in my voice.

"Maybe."

"That is *so* like him. He thinks I'm gonna waltz right over there and get myself killed. I'm not that stupid, Ambrose."

"I know that. But he didn't exactly say it that way."

"He didn't have to. Of course I'll wait for the police to come. Those two over there bludgeoned Charlotte to death. They obviously don't care what happens to anyone else. I know when to back off."

Ambrose shot me a look, but at least he didn't correct me.

"Seriously. I may have found out who killed Charlotte, but I don't want to become their next victim."

"I know this is hard for you. But we have to sit tight."

Both of us fell silent then. *What more is there to say?* The people responsible for Charlotte Devereaux's death sat only yards away, enjoying a leisurely meal. At a public restaurant, out in the open, with nowhere to hide. As far as they were concerned, life went on, and the toughest choice they faced now was what to order for dessert.

I began to fidget as I focused on the injustice of it all. I turned my head this way and that, taking it all in. When I craned my neck just so, I could barely see the back of Trudi's head over the old man's shoulder. Her brown hair glowed under the houselights, and it bobbed up and down a few times. No doubt she was wagging her finger at Barrett again, and her head kept time with the movement.

The third time it happened, Barrett suddenly leaped to his feet. He threw something down—no doubt his dinner napkin—and picked something else up from the table. His shoulders stretched taut against the pinstriped shirt as he lifted what looked like a notepad.

"Oh, shine!" I turned to Ambrose, my eyes widening. "He's got the dinner check. They're going to leave before Lance gets here!"

Unfortunately, Trudi rose as well, and casually tossed the mink over her shoulders. Instead of waiting for her fiancé, she stalked away from the table, the coat slipping sideways as she pushed past his chair.

It all happened so quickly. *Slam!* Something hit the wall behind me, and I turned to see three men barrel into the restaurant. Officer Hernandez came first with his gun drawn, followed by Lance, who wore the wrinkled khakis again. A third officer, one I didn't recognize, brought up the rear.

They rushed into the room as a hush fell over the tables. Lance didn't stop until he reached Trudi, who looked shocked to see him.

"Stop right there!" he commanded.

She stopped, but her coat continued to sway around her legs like a pendulum.

Meanwhile, I turned to see Barrett, who remained standing at the table, with the dinner check in his hand. He seemed to be weighing his options. He quickly tossed the bill down and then he darted in the opposite direction.

There was no time to react. Everything slowed as he zigged past the elderly couple and then zagged around the family of four. Just when I thought he'd pass us in a blur, Ambrose grabbed onto the edge of our table and stuck out his leg.

Crash!

Barrett never saw it coming. Once he smacked into Bo's shin, he tumbled end over end, until his head struck the floor with a *thwack*. His body went limp and his face contorted in pain.

My gaze flew forward again. Now Trudi stood with her hands pinned behind her back. The officer I didn't know had widened her stance by nudging her feet apart, while Lance withdrew a pair of handcuffs from his pocket. She didn't resist when he slapped them on her wrists.

Meanwhile, Officer Hernandez must've heard the commotion by our table, because he sprinted toward us. When he arrived, he bent over the carpet and grabbed something on his utility belt. Once he secured some handcuffs around Barrett's wrists, he turned him right-side-up on the carpet and shouted something to me.

"Who's this?"

"That's Barrett Hudson, her fiancé." I couldn't look at the injured man. "They were both involved in the murder."

"Need any help, Officer?" Ambrose half-rose from his chair.

"Nah. I've got this one." The policeman hoisted Barrett to his feet, who reacted with a loud moan.

All three policemen marched their prisoners to the front of the restaurant. When Trudi saw her fiancé in handcuffs, she snarled at him.

Poor Barrett... he doesn't stand a chance. She'd turn on him faster than a cobra strike.

"What's going on around here?" It was Odilia, who huffed up to our table, her cheeks pink from running. She clutched a wine bottle for a weapon.

"We found out who killed Charlotte." I spoke quickly. There was no time for a lengthy explanation, since she looked ready to bean someone. "I called Lance. They got them both in custody."

We all turned to stare at the spectacle. Somehow, Trudi managed to look haughty, even with a police officer on either side of her and the fur coat all askew.

"But they're our customers." Clearly, Odilia had no idea who was dining in her restaurant that night. To her, Trudi and Barrett were like any other dinner guests, only ones who happened to be in handcuffs at the moment.

"I'm afraid so." I glanced at Ambrose, who carefully massaged his shin, obviously in pain. "Are you okay, Bo?"

"Yah." He continued to nurse the leg. "Just glad that guy didn't get away."

"That was very brave of you."

"Brave, schmave. I figured there was only one way to stop that guy, and I didn't want you to be the one to do it."

"Oh, Bo." I thought about swatting his arm, but only for a moment, since he'd been injured enough for one night.

"Who are they?" Odilia asked.

"That's Trudi Whidbee and her fiancé. She hired Charlotte Devereaux to plan her wedding." I gently lifted Ambrose's hand off his leg so I could take over. "Only Charlotte ended up having an affair with that guy."

"I knew it! I knew a man was involved somehow." She sounded vindicated. "Two women like Bettina and Charlotte don't go at it like they did unless it involves a man."

"You were right," I said. "And this man was supposed to marry someone else." I finished rubbing Ambrose's shin. "Can we go home now?"

"There's only one problem." He glanced around our empty table. "We never did get anything to eat, and you look ready to faint."

"Really? After everything that's happened, you're worried about me having dinner?"

"Sure," he said. "Lance has those two in custody, and we can't do anything else until we go to the police station to give our statement."

Odilia broke in. "I know what to do. I'll have one of my busboys send some food over to your house. You're both goin' to have a long night tonight."

"She's right, you know." Ambrose slowly rose and then helped me to my feet. "We'll have to go down to the police station and it might take a while. It seems like we've been there way too much lately."

I managed a grin, even with the chaos. By now, Trudi and Barrett were gone; muscled through the front door by Lance and the other officers. The air around us began to buzz again, as people started to whisper about what they'd seen.

I took it all in, my view tempered by exhaustion. "One thing you can say about our dates, Ambrose. They're never boring."

He grinned and clutched my waist. We both waved good-bye to Odilia, and then we began to walk away from the table. Our steps were wobbly because of Ambrose's injured leg, but we still managed to cover some ground. At the last moment, I glanced over my shoulder and saw Odilia place the wine bottle on the table.

"Just a second." I gently slipped out from his grasp and worked my way back to her.

"Did you forget something?" she asked.

"I figured we'd take that wine to go, if you don't mind." I pointed to the bottle on the table. "We could use it after the night we've had."

"Of course. Here you go." She gave me the bottle, along with a wink.

Did Odilia really just wink at me? My nerves were so shot, I couldn't trust my eyes at this point. Regardless, she looked tickled to see me take the bottle and return to Ambrose, who waited for me by the entrance to the foyer.

"So that's what brought you back there," he said, as soon as he noticed my hand.

"I wanted to make sure we have everything we need tonight. There's no telling how long we'll be with Lance, but at least we can look forward to going home again."

We took a few more steps toward the exit when Ambrose suddenly stopped. "Do you hear anything?"

"No, not really."

"Shhh. Listen. It sounds like music. Piano music."

I cocked my head toward the sound. Sure enough, a few lilting notes reached me, over the buzz of conversation. It *was* piano music and it was coming from the foyer. A familiar tune, maybe Bach or Beethoven.

We stepped closer to the foyer. Definitely Bach. Someone was playing the opening strains of "Jesu, Joy of Man's Desiring."

I peered around the corner. Prudence Fortenberry sat at the piano in the foyer, still in her faux-fur coat, which meant she must have just arrived. She used her left hand to play the lower part of the keyboard, while her injured right hand lay in her lap.

A few folks milled around the upright and listened to her play.

When she finished, I left Ambrose's side and moved over to her. "Hello, Prudence."

She looked at me vaguely, her eyes bleary. "Hi, Missy. I didn't even see you there. I kind of get wrapped up in the music when I'm playing."

"I could tell. It's a beautiful piece. I'm sorry I ever told that bride it was overused. I apologize."

"Pshaw." She casually waved her good hand. "To be honest, it *is* overdone. Almost a cliché now."

One by one, the strangers around us wandered away as Prudence and I continued our conversation. Even Ambrose kept his distance, no doubt to provide us some privacy.

"So, what are you doing here?" I asked.

"Testing the piano. Odilia wants me to start playing here on Friday nights. Said it'll be a good way to entertain folks while they wait in line." She waved again, but this time with her injured hand. "Of course, I can't start yet. But, at least I could check out the instrument to see if it's been tuned."

"That's a wonderful idea! About you playing, I mean. I've been here on a Friday night before, and it's packed to the gills."

"No one ever books me for weddings then, anyway. Might as well make some money on my downtime." She swiveled around. "What brings you here?"

"I was having dinner with Ambrose Jackson."

"Ooohhh . . . I've met him several times. You should wrap that one up and take him home."

"I know, right? There was a big commotion here tonight, and we were just leaving."

"Commotion?"

"The police left a few minutes ago. They got the people responsible for Charlotte's death."

Prudence gasped. "Do tell! Who in the world would do that to our sweet Charlotte?"

"It was Trudi Whidbee, along with her fiancé. They're on their way to the police station right now."

"I hate to say it, but it makes perfect sense." Prudence leaned in. "That girl was downright ugly to me when she found out about my hand. She fired me on the spot. Said she couldn't risk losing me for her precious wedding if it didn't heal in time. Can you imagine? Talk about overreacting."

"Now that you mention it . . ." I leaned in too, since what I was about to ask wasn't meant for others to hear. "Whatever happened to your hand? That's a nasty injury."

"This?" She gave a forced laugh. "It's kind of embarrassing, to tell you the truth. I got too close to the blades in the garbage disposal. Dropped my ring down the drain and just panicked." She turned the injured hand over in her lap. "Could've been a whole lot worse, though. Turns out the blade only grazed it and didn't cut anything major. Pretty much a surface wound, even though it looks nasty as heck."

"Whew." My eyes widened. "You're incredibly lucky. Who knows what could've happened."

"Tell me about it. That's the first and last time I'll ever dive after jewelry like that again."

By now, Ambrose had decided it was safe to enter the conversation, and he appeared at my side. He carefully took Prudence's left hand in his. "Nice to see you again. You play beautifully. Even with only one hand."

"Pshaw. That's sweet of you to say. Come back in a few weeks, and you'll hear some real piano playing. I'll be here every Friday night, from seven p.m. to midnight."

"Got it. We really should get going, though, Missy. Lance will want us at the police station soon."

"Do tell." Curiosity blazed in Prudence's eyes. "Were you the ones who caught them?"

"No, not really." I spoke quickly, eager to dispel any misinformation. Since Prudence knew almost everyone in town, she was an important cog in the rumor mill. "The police officers took them into custody. Let's give the police all the credit for getting those two off the streets."

"I agree," she said. "Makes me thankful for our boys in blue."

Ambrose shifted beside me, which meant he was growing impatient. But, something else nagged at my memory, refusing to be ignored. "One last thing. Remember when we met up in the parking lot this morning?"

"Yeah, when I got your skirt all muddy, right? Didn't I give you enough money for the dry cleaner?"

"No, it's not that. It's something else. I kinda peeked inside your car when you ducked inside to get some money. It was packed to the roof. I thought you might be leaving us for a while."

She smiled. "Well, I can see why you'd think that. My car must've looked a sight. I had to clean house, and it turns out I have way too much sheet music. I like to donate my extras to the high school choir department. They're so short of funds, you know."

"But, I also saw suitcases in there."

"Those were empty ones. I gave them to the choir director. He said they take an annual trip to a music festival—I think it's Dallas this year—and not all the kids have decent luggage."

No wonder she carried so much stuff in her car. "I'm so sorry I badgered you, then. And, it's wonderful you donate to the school."

"You didn't badger me. I can see why you might be confused."

"Uh, Missy?" Ambrose took hold of my elbow again. "We really should get going."

"You're right. We'll see you soon, Prudence. Don't let anything else happen to your hands. It sounds like Odilia needs you here at her restaurant."

We left her sitting at the piano, with her right hand still in her lap. By the time we walked through the exit, she'd begun one of Bach's preludes, and music once more filled the foyer.

Chapter 23

As we drove away from the restaurant, both Ambrose and I retreated into silence. Every once in a while, he snuck a glance at me as we drove down Highway 18, which I pretended not to notice.

Who knew he and I would visit Odilia's restaurant for a quiet meal, only to watch the police apprehend the couple responsible for Charlotte's murder? Not only that, but the culprits turned out to be a former client and her erstwhile fiancé, which made it even more surreal.

I could only imagine what was taking place at the police station while we drove. By now, Lance would have Trudi sequestered in the nondescript interview room, a place clearly beneath her, which she'd tell him in no uncertain terms. She might even insist he release her *this very instant.* When Lance didn't comply, she'd ask to call her daddy's high-priced attorney, and then they'd wait, in stony silence, for the man to arrive.

Meanwhile, Barrett would squirm in a different conference room down the hall, his physical pain nothing compared to the psychological wringer he was about to go through. He had to know his fiancée would rat him out. We all did. It was only a matter of time.

After a few more minutes, Ambrose finally broke the silence. "That's strange."

The Sweetwater mansion appeared in the windshield up ahead, its roofline dark against the night sky. Now, however, several lights blazed in the windows on the first floor, and the front door stood wide open.

"You're right . . . that's really weird." I forgot about everything else for a moment as the mansion drew near. Sure enough, I could see all the way from the porch into where the grand staircase stood.

"Do you think Hank knows he left his front door open?" Ambrose asked.

"I don't know. I don't see any movement in the house."

He slowed the car and then pulled over to the shoulder of the road. Hank's white pickup sat in its usual spot by the mansion, right next to the kitchen, but there was no sign of Hank.

"He's definitely home," I said. "Could be he just forgot to close the front door."

"Maybe."

"Either way, we should tell him." I quickly glanced at the clock on the Audi's dash. Only ten minutes had passed since the chaotic scene at Miss Odilia's Southern Eatery.

"Are you sure Lance won't mind?"

"He'll forgive us if we only take a second." I knew at some point Lance would expect us at the police station, and we might as well get his questions over with. But that didn't mean I could ignore Hank's dilemma. He'd do anything for me, even donate the shirt off his back—albeit one in god-awful colors—and he'd do the same for anyone else in Bleu Bayou. I couldn't pretend he didn't need our help now. "C'mon, Ambrose. Let's make sure he's okay."

Ambrose reluctantly turned off the ignition and left the Audi. The minute I stepped outside too, a strange feeling washed over me.

"Whoa." I waited for it to pass, as I picked my way along the pea-gravel path to the mansion. "Didn't see that coming."

Ambrose walked two steps ahead of me, but he slowed. "What now?" he asked over his shoulder. "Did you see something?"

"No. But I had the strangest feeling of déjà vu. Like we were just here."

"That's because we *were* just here. Remember? It was two days ago. We came to Mr. Dupre's New Year's Day breakfast."

"That's right! It seems like weeks ago."

I hurried to catch up with him, my arms flailing as I jogged. That was when I remembered the wine bottle in my hand, which I still held. "Did you say something else? I can't hear you."

He came to a dead stop. "I said someone should've eaten the damn peas that day."

"Hold the phone. Are you telling me you think this is all my fault?"

By now, we stood on the front porch, in a rectangle of light that poured through the front door.

"Maybe. Would it have killed you to eat the good-luck peas?"

"For goodness sakes, Ambrose. Just for that, I won't share the wine with you."

I flashed the bottle at him before he could protest and hurried through the front door. Sure enough, a crystal chandelier above my head threw prisms of light around the empty room. My favorite part of the house actually lay beneath me: beautiful mahogany hardwoods that glimmered like pond water under my feet.

"Mr. Dupre?" My voice echoed in the stillness.

Ambrose arrived a second later. He looked befuddled too when no one answered my call.

"*Hhheeellllooo?*" I tried again, my voice once more bouncing around the room. After a moment, I tiptoed to the end of the foyer and stuck my head in the hall.

Several rooms branched off the foyer, including a dining room, sitting area and kitchen, way out in the back. I made my way to the dining room first, where I spied something by the fireplace.

It was Hank Dupre, who had brought one of the dining room chairs close to the fireplace. His chin rested on his chest and his eyes were half-closed, as he softly snored by the flames. The fire that danced over the logs couldn't compete with the bright orange golf shirt he wore.

Footsteps sounded behind me, so I turned and pressed my finger to my lips. "Shhhh. He's sleeping."

I inched closer to him and heard another snore. I was about to touch his arm, when his eyes flew open. "Wah?"

"Hi, Mr. Dupre. It's me. Missy DuBois. You left your front door open."

He quickly straightened. "Missy?"

"Yes, and Ambrose Jackson is here too." Thankfully, he didn't tease me about calling him Hank this time. "We drove by your property and saw you'd left your front door open. We didn't want anything bad to happen to you."

"I left it open?" He still looked confused, but at least the wariness was gone. "First time that's ever happened."

"It's okay . . . we closed it for you." Ambrose had joined us by the fireplace. "We knew you were home, so we figured you just forgot."

"Guess my old age is catching up with me," he said. "I'm grateful you two happened to come along."

I reached for a different dining chair, after first setting the wine bottle on the floor, and took a seat next to him. The poor man needed a moment to wake up. "We were glad to help you. You'd do the same for us."

"Darn right I would." His gaze traveled to the floor. "What'd you bring me?"

"Huh?" I followed his eyes. *Dadgummit.* So much for a romantic evening sharing a bottle of wine with Ambrose. I couldn't very well take the bottle back now without hurting his feelings. "Miss Odilia gave it to me. It's from her restaurant."

"That was nice of her. Is it your birthday?"

"No." I glanced over to Ambrose, who shrugged. "But we *are* celebrating tonight. Lance LaPorte got the people who murdered Charlotte Devereaux."

Hank's mouth rounded to a perfect O. "You don't say! Who was it?"

"Two people you might not know: one of the brides who originally hired Charlotte to plan her wedding and her fiancé. Everything went bad when the fiancé got a little too close to the wedding planner. They killed her afterward and then tried to hide the body in a whiskey barrel."

"That's incredible."

"There's more." I scooted a bit closer to the fire, grateful for its warmth. "At one point, I actually thought Paxton Haney might've killed her. Now I know he had nothing to do with it."

"Why'd you suspect him?"

"Because he told me he wanted to sell the business. Who sells a business only a few days after a partner dies?"

Hank crossed his arms. "I would have explained it to you, if you asked me."

Was that a reprimand? I couldn't quite read his expression in the half-light, but the tone definitely sounded parental. "I'm sorry. I should've done that. But . . . why did he ask you to help him sell the business so soon after Charlotte died?"

"Because he was devastated. He couldn't imagine running the business without her."

"He told me he wanted to retire," I said. "But Charlotte wouldn't let him."

"That was a ruse. He loved that business deep down. But he didn't think he could run it on his own. And he was so frustrated about the murder, since there weren't any suspects right away. He had to do *something* to keep his mind occupied, to keep himself from going crazy. So, cleaning up his records and listing the business gave him something to do."

My memory reeled back to the day before, when I spied him shredding bank statements. "There's something I don't understand. I happened to see him in his office this morning. He was shredding papers. Lots of papers. And they were statements from the local bank."

"Good. He listened to what I told him."

"Come again?" I couldn't imagine any real estate agent would advise a client to shred records. Especially not so close to a sale.

"Those were duplicates, Missy. The man was a pack rat. Sheridan was always trying to get him to consolidate. Guess it finally sunk in."

Ah, the accountant. "So those were only duplicates?"

"Of course. Both Sheridan and I told him he had to do a clean sweep. Otherwise, he'd scare off any potential buyers."

Ambrose stepped behind my chair and laid a hand on my shoulder. "I hate to say this . . . but we should probably get going. Lance will need us down at the station, and we should let Mr. Dupre here finish his nap."

"Nah." He waved away Ambrose's comment. "I'm good. Just grateful you two came along when you did."

"No problem, Mr. Dupre."

He shot me a funny look.

Since I knew exactly what was coming next, I beat him to the punch. "I know, I know. It's Hank. Mr. Dupre is your dad."

"You got that right."

I couldn't help but smile. "I just realized something. This is where it all started. The three of us, just two days ago. Right here in this dining room."

Hank and Ambrose glanced at each other, and then they both opened their mouths to speak. "Next time, eat the good-luck peas!" they said in unison.

Sandra Bretting has served as a freelance feature writer for the *Houston Chronicle* since moving to Texas in 1996. She received a journalism degree from the University of Missouri School of Journalism, and spent her early career in health-care public relations at medical centers throughout Southern California. Other publications for which she's written include the *Los Angeles Times* and *Woman's Day*. Readers can visit her website at www.SandraBretting.com.

MURDER AT
MORNINGSIDE

A Missy DuBois Mystery

First in a
New Series!

SANDRA BRETTING

SOMETHING
FOUL AT
SWEETWATER

A Missy DuBois Mystery

SANDRA
BRETTING

Printed in the United States
by Baker & Taylor Publisher Services